I0637020

STEEL MACHINES

STEEL MACHINES

DAN FRANKLIN

CEMETERY DANCE PUBLICATIONS

Baltimore
2025

Copyright © 2025 by Dan Franklin

All rights reserved. No part of this book may be reproduced in any form or by any electronic or mechanical means, including information storage and retrieval systems, without permission in writing from the publisher, except by a reviewer who may quote brief passages in a review.

Cemetery Dance Publications
132-B Industry Lane, Unit #7
Forest Hill, MD 21050
http://www.cemeterydance.com

The characters and events in this book are fictitious.
Any similarity to real persons, living or dead,
is coincidental and not intended by the author.

Trade Paperback Edition Printing

ISBN: 978-1-964780-40-5

Cover Artwork and Design © 2025 by Vincent Chong
Interior Art © 2025 by Dan Franklin, Vincent Cong, and Jamie Stearns
Interior Design © 2025 by Desert Isle Design, LLC

Dedicated to my wife Kelsey
and my children, Layla and Marshall
To those with hearts like steel machines
And to all those who survive.

Though I than He - may longer live
He longer must - than I -
For I have but the power to kill,
Without - the power to die -

—Emily Dickenson,
My Life Had Stood, A Loaded Gun

CHAPTER 1

OTTO woke to the sound of boots on the floor of the foyer below and even before his eyes had fully opened, he knew the nightmare had at last spilled over into reality.

His parents were already awake, their panic broadcast through the darkness in the quiet rustle of hushed words and hurried movements—muffled white-noise sounds that did nothing to mask the steady thump-thump-thump from below that thundered in time with the rhythm of his heart. His pajamas tangled around him as he struggled half upright.

The footsteps reached the stairwell and began to climb.

"We have to do something," his mother whispered. "You have to stop them."

"It'll protect us." His father's voice was a low rumble in the dark. "This is what it was made to do. I built it for a reason."

"It isn't real! It's just a pile of junk!" Her desperation carried an electricity to it, sent a prickle like centipede legs across the greasy mop of hair that covered Otto's scalp.

Otto pawed the sleep from his eyes, squinted to find familiar shapes in the faint candlewick glow. As cramped as the attic was, the shadows still managed to swallow the light. The steeply pitched roofing allowed for a single small window high above him, but any glow from the moon that might have found its way through the shutters was choked in clouds, and only the winter chill leeched in. The night shivered in anticipation as the flame stirred.

"Papa?" Otto asked.

His father hushed him, slashed his finger in the air as if silence would do any good, a familiar movement that Otto sensed more than saw. The men below had come various times before, but never like this. Not idle wandering or inspection, this time. Now they moved with purpose.

Otto's mother hunched close by, a vulture's silhouette. Her hand found his and squeezed, but the clammy dampness of her palms granted only a meager scrap of comfort. Her breath was sour, the sweaty warmth of her skin held an almost feverish intensity. He huddled closer just the same.

His father, gaunt face lost among the tangle of beard and shadow, turned away from them, toward the sprawling heap piled up against the wall. Toward the monstrosity he'd built, that he'd been building for the last three years.

"You need to have faith," he said. "Faith and will."

The footsteps reached the top of the staircase.

Otto's vision still hadn't fully adjusted but he could imagine his father's creation clearly, every detail in sharp relief, as familiar as either of his parents. He'd seen it every day, watched it develop from a skeletal frame into the hulking form it now held, a crazed collection of cogs and gears, corrugated sheet metal and welded wire that knelt on steel-capped legs yet still towered above them. Oversized brass-rimmed goggles made an approximation of eyes that glinted from up among the rafters. The open palms of its hands, forged from a car's chrome wheel caps and as large as Otto's torso, ended in fingers of soldered metal hangers and shoe-tips. They rested facing upwards on its steel-plated thighs in a universal gesture of penitent submission. Nails and bolts sprouted in a jagged forest from the joints, glinted among the symbols his father had etched into the scraps.

God built the first man from clay, Otto's father had told him once. *Wait and see what this can do.*

His papa fussed over the etchings, mumbling unfamiliar words as he toiled. Not the sort of Hebrew that Otto knew from his classes, at least. He'd heard his father practice it enough to recognize the sounds—a collection of glottal consonants that once made Otto think of tumbling rocks but now made him think of steel-wheeled train cars, of the ugly clack of guns fixing into position, of the rattling laugh of men with no mercy in their hearts.

Otto wondered how many of them were down there.

Impossible to say. It didn't really matter. Too many.

"Mama?" The squeak of his own voice ignited his terror.

"Hush, Otto."

"Mama, don't let them—"

The damp hand released his shoulder, clamped over his mouth instead. Her fingers gripped his jaw like a vise.

"Hush," she said again.

The candle snuffed out and the darkness was complete. The only sound left was his father, chanting his quiet, ugly words—not a language for men at all—and the parade of boots heading down the hall.

Into the library.

His father continued, but his voice quavered, and the strange sounds tumbled over each other and fell apart. He started again but Otto's mother cut him off.

"*Quiet!*"

At last Otto's father paused, held his breath. Otto did too. The hand across his mouth squeezed tighter, mashed his lips into his teeth until he could taste bitter blood.

The boots stopped. Muffled voices muttered below, confusion replacing the urgency of their ascent.

A stray bit of moonlight leaked in for a moment from the window above, gave a passing glimpse at the pitiful home that had been Otto's world for over two years. The bedsheets hanging from the rafters that divided the open floor into rooms to give the illusion of space. The mattress with its dresser beside it became a bedroom. The dining room was a small table that they used for eating, an ugly little battery-powered radio sitting beside the candle. Most of the meals consisted of flatbread or crackers and cans of bland, murky soup. The bucket of human waste in the far corner was a bathroom, its stained wooden edge peeking through the gap in the curtain, the smell always slightly present, regardless of whether his father had freshly emptied and cleaned it in the toilet of the house below. Years reduced into monotonous, unyielding days with little to eat and less to do, colors extinguished one by one and seasons reduced to either the uncomfortable Prague summer heat or the infiltration of biting winter winds.

Otto had almost forgotten that there was another way to live, that there might be a life beyond flinching from footsteps and desperate late-night vigils in the dark. The threat of the voices below paused for just long enough for him to feel ashamed.

When the clouds once more swallowed the moonlight, Otto breathed a sigh of relief.

The men couldn't find them. Not like this, not tonight, not now. Not so helpless. It wasn't right. It wasn't fair. They'd done everything his father had said to do. The war was supposed to be ending soon—both his parents agreed on that, and these days they agreed on so few things. His body felt puny, strengthless, pathetically weak. His bladder spasmed and warmth spilled down his thighs in a wet rush, and he wanted to cry but knew it wouldn't do any good. He wondered if those men below could hear the suffocating crash of his heartbeat through the ceiling.

Silence reigned downstairs. They hadn't left. Otto could feel them, could detect their presence in a simple instinctive awareness that wasn't tied to any particular sense. They were waiting, then. Searching.

A tiny metallic clink—a spring or screw or something—gave a musical tinkle as it toppled among the trays and plates and armor of the makeshift man, thudded to the ground and rolled, impossibly loud in the stillness.

Otto squeezed his eyes shut despite the darkness. His pajama pants clung wetly to his thighs, already growing cold. He tried to pray, but he couldn't remember how, couldn't think of anything beyond: *We're not here we're not here we're not here.*

Something thumped to the floor in the room below as if in answer. Then another thump, and another. Books, torn from shelves and thrown aside, swept clear from the bookcase that stood as the final barrier between them and the men. Movement again, voices, and louder this time. The sound of metal biting into the shelves, tearing into the wall. The first streak of artificial light slipped through the cracks like water through the hull, and then the men below began bellowing, the braying of dogs with cornered prey.

Crrrrrack.

Otto's father began praying in earnest, his incantation rising like a song, but his voice broke and the words became a plea instead of a command. The metal man did nothing.

Otto's mother let go of Otto, darted toward the creation and crouched beside it. She wrenched part of the plating back and gestured at the dark hollow inside.

"In," she said to him. "Go. Now, Otto. Run!"

Otto gave one last glance at his father, but the man ignored him. His hands were flung up above his head and he shouted something, an unfamiliar, ugly phrase. Then Otto obeyed his mother and scurried over, threw himself into the breach headfirst, squirmed and grunted as she pushed him deeper in among the spiderwebs and grease and dust that clung to his teeth and stung his eyes, pushed him harder against the jagged edges that clawed at his skin. She pressed the plating back into place and then Otto could only see through a small gap in the baking sheets that made up the metal man's belly.

The men poured up the stairwell in a wave of electric light and sound, their uniforms a dull slate gray. The color of iron. The weapons in their hands looked cut from the night. The attic lit up like noon.

His father turned to the intruders, snarled the words again, and was answered by the crack of a gunshot.

He hit the ground, one hand grasping at his throat. Blood spurted through his fingers, spilled out in a rush, pooled beneath him as he twitched and kicked and shook. His eyes rolled, wide with panic, until they found Otto's and there they stayed, staring back through the gap at the boy. His hand relaxed before his expression went slack. The halo of a flashlight's beam crowned his face, a face Otto had seen laugh and weep, smile and frown, only now the slate was clean. His father's face, no more than a mask. A flawed imitation.

Two boots, black with polish, planted themselves next to the body and then the shooter crouched down.

Otto's mind was as paralyzed as his body, and he watched without comprehension as the man inspected his father, noted the dead man's gaze, and then followed it until he was looking in, through the gap. His eyes widened in surprise, but then his smile did too. His teeth looked like pale stones among the shadow. The man opened his mouth and then someone stepped in beside him. A hammer lodged itself, claw end first, in the middle of his face with a wet, hollow slap.

Otto's mother gripped the hammer handle, jerked it upwards and then the back of her head blew out and she toppled, stiff-bodied, to the floor.

Sound receded beyond a shrilling that burrowed through Otto's ears and into his brain. Chaos and the jumping flashlights strobed across him, across the attic, poured their dizzying confusion down his throat in a drowning wave.

His mother.

She'd held his hand in the field at Letna Park, pressed the wheel of a kite into his grip. The line tugged, snapped, jerked as the red sail heaved its way up into a flawlessly blue sky, the kind of blue that artists painted pictures of, the kind potters stained their wares, the kind of blue he'd seen in synagogue drawings of ancient kings. For that one perfect moment he'd stared upwards in awe, his mouth open, the spring wind licking around his neck as the kite pulled on him and he felt as if it might lift him up after it. As if the straining cord was a direct tether between him and some sentient, cosmic force instead of simple wind. In that moment he'd believed in God and love and forever and any good thing that offered itself. Then the kite yanked its way out of his hand and he'd laughed and chased after it and she'd run with him as it sailed across the open rolling field of yarrow and daisy-speckled green and toward the Vltava River beyond.

He squeezed his eyes shut and held onto the image, but it did nothing to dampen the hot stench of oil and smoke and cordite. He tried not to move. Not to think. And still the night leaked in.

The flurry of activity continued on, barely more than an arm's reach away, but he didn't open his eyes to watch as they barked their commands and raced around. The man with the ruined face howled and whimpered, his voice slurry with fluid as they helped him down the stairs.

—the hammer sprouted from the middle of his face, the claw bit in just below his nose. That wet crack was his skull unlatching—

Most of them left with the wounded man, from the sounds of it, but a few stayed behind. Two, he supposed. Maybe three. Otto could hear them grunt with exertion as they dragged twin burdens toward the stairwell, and then the heavy tumbling thuds that answered.

They did not speak as they knocked over furniture, tore cloth, rummaged about. The radio shattered with a musical crash. Table legs snapped. They had no need for words. The destruction was a methodical, mechanical process they'd clearly performed countless times before.

And then when those footsteps retreated too, Otto finally opened his eyes to find a single man standing in the middle of the room. Unlike the iron gray of the others, he wore black. A band, the color of blood, gripped one arm. The glowing tip of a cigarette danced in front of his face.

The bodies of Otto's parents were gone.

They threw them down the stairs. Dragged them off. Gone. Like smoke.

Whisps leaked from the corners of the man's mouth as he panned his flashlight across the metal construct, as if some terrible fire guttered and burned within him. A blaze of illumination glinted through the gaps in the metal armor, razor-edged starlight cutting through into the dark cage where Otto huddled. Otto's breath fluttered—shallow, soundless gulps of air that stank of violence. The world spun on a bent axis, twisting senselessly. His mind snapped blank. Empty of prayer. Of hope. He simply waited, a feral animal frozen in place by the majesty of inescapable death. The flashlight's beam climbed to the face of the metal man. To the smooth, dispassionate expression that Otto knew too well.

Like the face of his father. The face of a corpse.

The face of God.

Otto held as still as he could, glad he'd wet himself earlier because now he had nothing left. He held his breath as the killer watched, waited, just beyond the thin divide of metal. There was nowhere left to run.

The smoking man unslung his gun and raised it and Otto had a single moment to hope it was an empty threat before he opened fire. The attic reduced to a strobe of blinding light and a hammering blast of sound so loud that Otto thought he must have screamed, but the sound was flattened beneath the cannonade. Beaten metal dimpled against Otto, formed spikes that pressed through his nightshirt as bullets whined and plinked, some caught in the metal, some ricocheting freely. Something tugged at his ear, left a stinging white flare of lightning that seared his jaw, but then the gunfire stopped.

The metal man sagged, bowed under its own weight and collapsed, taking Otto with it. The plating peeled back like the lid of a can and his cheek smacked against the wood panels of the floor. Split metal dug into his ribs with cruel, jagged teeth as some piece of the construct squeezed the air out of him. He did not dare try to raise his head, could only watch in stunned terror through the exposed opening as the flashlight swept down toward him, but the light caught the smoke and caused the air between them to glow, reduced the killer to little more than an inhuman silhouette.

The figure bellowed a laugh, turned, and left.

Otto's ears rang too sharply for him to distinguish the footfalls, but the vibrations of the bootsteps on the floorboards faded. Without the flashlights, there was nothing much to see by. There was nothing to see. The red gave way to black. Merciful darkness reigned supreme.

Otto wasn't sure how long he waited, barely breathing. Time lost its footing, the world itself blurring as if he were trapped in some nightmarish middle ground between reality and confusion that might never quite loose its jaws. Finally, when he couldn't stand the pain of the weight pressing down on him, he planted his hands and pushed himself upward with what feeble strength he could manage.

For a moment, he wondered if he would be able to escape at all, or if he'd stay trapped inside the metal cage until he was just one more corpse, but the fall had jarred the gears loose and he managed to drag himself through the wreckage. His fingers gripped rungs and cogs as he crawled, brushed their way through the tattered copper jackets of bullets, their heat long spent.

He squeezed his way out and rolled onto his back, stared up at the shutter-shrouded window. The haze had dissipated, some. Enough to make out the desolation by the scraps of moonlight.

His parents were gone. Even their bodies were gone. His home was demolished, reduced to a violated shell of ruin and death. The golem lay in a broken heap, hands and legs splayed, head fully detached.

Yimakh shemo

His father had shouted it, and destruction had followed. Otto didn't remember ever learning the words in any of his lessons, but he understood what it meant. His father had issued a command to the construct.

And it had done nothing.

"*Yimakh shemo,*" Otto whispered. Not simply to kill, as he knew other words for that—*ratsach* and *harag* and even *shamad*—but to destroy completely. To let their name and memory be forever erased.

Something shifted among the heap. Not just the ruination settling either. The sound was deliberate, the creaking groan of effort. It took Otto only a moment to locate the source: the golem's hand. No longer did it rest, palm open, in the center of the pooled blood his father had left behind. No longer did it signal its acceptance.

It was clenched into a fist.

CHAPTER 2

TTO waited beside the clenched fist until long after the sun began to stream in through the roof window, replacing the clouds and night with a dull midday glow.

He wasn't sure how many hours had passed, or if he had slept. It might as well have been a lifetime slipping by. The sulfur stink of gun smoke remained heavy in the air, sharp and metallic, indivisible from the scent of blood. His ribs still throbbed, but his ear had crusted over, felt oddly heavy. Thinking took a physical effort, a struggle against a heavy, clouding mental fog.

The attic was a disaster.

The cramped little fragment of home had been stripped of what warmth it could muster, of love and life and comfort. Now it existed as stained wooden planks, a ceiling of rafters holding up the high-angled pitch of the roof. The curtains that had divided the open space into makeshift rooms—the bathroom with its bucket, his father's corner workshop, the shared mattress where they slept—all had been torn down and thrown in stomped, tangled lumps reminiscent of shrouded corpses. There was nothing left to hide the destruction.

The rug was stamped with boot prints and speckled in a fine dusting of red. The small dresser, its drawers open and hanging like tongues from a panting dog, stood among a pool of torn clothing. The lamp that had once sat on it, that had once meant something to his parents, lay in a broken heap. Otto couldn't remember the significance or if he'd ever seen it turned on. The table had been stripped of its legs, and the radio smashed beside it. The storage chest had been kicked to splinters, rifled through, the contents in a ruined pile of crushed candles, dented cans, the tattered pages of books. Bags hung from hooks on the wall, mostly undisturbed, but even they looked malnourished and depleted. The men who had looted the place had been in a hurry, or they might have gotten to them too, Otto supposed.

He picked up a small white chunk of debris from the ground and inspected it.

—in the flashes of gunfire, Otto saw the man's eyes rolling, wet and white and fluttering. Twin fissures ran from where the hammer bit into his face and filled with a rush of blood that seemed nearly black in the shadows. Something clicked across the ground, the last thing Otto heard before the gunshot—

A tooth.

He snatched his hand away from the bony fragment and wiped his fingers on the pants of his pajamas. Dull blue, drawstringed things with patched knees that his mother had replaced each winter, pants that had slowly transitioned from being hopelessly oversized to barely reaching halfway down his shin. He couldn't remember putting them on the night before. That life seemed to have slipped under and been all but lost in the avalanche of fire and death, only the barest remnants poking through the haze the killers had left behind.

His father's toolbox—a chipped metal chest, wagon-red and glossy and entirely at odds with the rest of the weathered attic—lay on its side, the latch broken and lid yawning open. A steely halo of screws and nails and wrenches and oddly shaped screwdrivers lay around it, glinting in the glow that crept in from the small round window above.

An inventor's kit. His father had been a clockmaker by trade, but his passion had been building, designing, studying. Creating.

He glanced, instinctively, toward the source of the light.

The wooden slats of the blinds that had been fixed across it were angled upward to keep anyone from seeing in, and the only parts of Prague visible were the tips of the houses, sharp-angled roofs at medieval pitches above an alabaster city. In the distance, one spire rose above the rest, but Otto couldn't make out any details. He didn't need to. He knew what it was.

"That," his father said, "is the Orloj. The greatest thing humanity ever designed."

"It's a clock?" Otto knew the answer. He had listened to the distant, glossy toll every day of his life. He gave the same answer anytime his papa mentioned the building, sensing somehow that his father hoped he'd forgotten every other time it was mentioned, so that he could reveal it for the first time once more.

His father let out a bark of laughter. "Is the ocean a pond? It tells more than time. It tells everything. The position of the planets and stars, the year, when the sun will set and the phase of the moon. Everything we've learned about time is in that clock. It has figures carved into it that caution against greed and lust and vanity, others that celebrate the timelessness of virtue. It's a marvel of the world, one of the most beautiful creations mankind ever constructed. Every hour, on the hour, Death strikes the bell and all those carvings shake their head to ask for more time. Thousands of years of humanity all lead to that."

Otto thought it looked like any other building, just a bit taller, but his dad thought it was marvel, so it was marvel. "Did you make it?" he asked, his voice barely more than a whisper.

His father let out a started chuckle, more genuine than before, and ruffled his hair.

"No. It's been around for five hundred years. No one has ever made anything greater. Yet. But give me time." He looked at Otto and winked.

Now he was passionless. Now he was dead.

The ugly, brutish hulk behind him made a mockery of his father's promise.

Otto set his hand beside the golem's fist, touched the stain below those polished fingers that were as thick as his wrist. The floorboards were only slightly tacky, most of the moisture already absorbed into the wood. He supposed he would cry more soon, but nothing came for the moment. Tears wouldn't fix anything anyway.

Instead, he surveyed the wreckage from a different man's eyes. An older man's. The rafters were clogged in cobwebs that he'd never noticed before. His mother had spent so much time cleaning them and keeping the attic tidy that it seemed strange that he would only be able to see them now. Dust spiraled in dirty helixes through the meager slats of sunlight, settled on stale watermarks and age-bleached waste. He felt, oddly, as if he were looking at the attic for the first time in decades.

When the feeling had passed and he felt fully grounded, he inspected the golem instead. Survival was his mother's last gift. His father had left him something entirely different. The metal man no longer sat on its haunches, all proud and menacing and strong, but now slouched drunkenly among its own scattered pieces. The goggles that once imitated eyes stared ahead, yielded nothing. The writing on its forehead, the single word—*emét*—had been punctuated with twin bullet holes that deformed the final letter of Ivri script.

The golem was far too big for Otto to get back upright. Even if he could, the metal plating on the entire chest portion had been bent and dented beyond function, and the gears inside were all knocked out of alignment, for what little good they had done. The structure now looked crude and ugly and indecent. He doubted it would hold itself upright unless it were fully rebuilt, but the idea was an impossibly large task to consider. Simply standing was a challenge.

One of the bags hanging along the wall had the tin of the crackers they shared for breakfast, and he chewed on a piece. It tasted like sawdust. He wondered how long the food would last him before he

The Prague Orloj

had to seek out more. Another task too big to consider. He touched the next bag over, felt the lumps of wood inside, but he didn't bother opening it.

His mother had carved and painted a small collection of toys to help him pass the hours, wooden blocks turned into cars, horses, figurines of men, and for the last year they'd been the most treasured items in his world, tucked carefully away each night inside the thick burlap.

You can be anything you imagine, his mother had told him, once, when he asked for more. *You've already got everything you need. You should be grateful.*

But that never stopped her from making more for him.

He eyed the bag with disinterest. The toys belonged to the Otto of yesterday. He didn't understand them anymore, couldn't fathom the hours of joy they'd brought. They weren't knights, dragons, cars and trains. They were just hunks of wood bolted together. He wasn't grateful, he didn't need them, and his imagination couldn't summon back what mattered. The world was too large for that, now. Too hollow.

The attic itself—which had felt torturously cramped since shortly after moving in—sprawled, grew wild in the shadows, as if the walls themselves fled the rusty, dirty pathway that the men had left behind.

The path leading downward.

As he stood at the top of the stairwell, he thought he could hear them. His mother, his father, voices far below. The sounds of cooking, of music and life and laughter and careless joy, but then the moment passed and it was quiet again. The doorway at the bottom was open.

Down the wooden plank stairs he went. He held onto the railing lining the wall, tried to fight back the waves of dizziness that broke against him.

The library had taken surprisingly little damage. The door to the hallway hung askew, letting light flood in. The bookshelf doorway had been wrenched off its sliding track, and the floor was littered with books and the pages from inside them that had been torn out and strewn about, but the carpet was only a little dirty and the piano looked untouched. Otto didn't dare touch it. He barely remembered the few lessons his mother had taught him way back when he was barely old enough to reach the keys. Silence had been more important than music for too many years.

Instead, he set to work cleaning up. Now that it was empty of books, the bookcase was light enough that he could slide it back into position. The hinges were still broken and it wouldn't open or close as smoothly as it used to, but it should be able to separate just far enough for him to slip in and out until he pulled it back into position. He could replace the bolt some other time. He gathered the loose pages from the floor and set them back inside the least mangled of the books and tucked them up onto the shelves. He wasn't sure why he bothered, but he supposed his mother would be proud and that was good enough for him.

He could so easily imagine the ghost of her tidying alongside him, the warmth of her smile, the tilt of her narrow chin, the smooth cascade of dark hair over her shoulders. Her quiet humming as she set each piece into place, dusted, prettied up a room that only they would see. He hummed along too for a moment, as he worked alongside her memory, but then he stopped.

He frowned.

His mother's hair was curly, wasn't it? Not straight. Something else was different about the thought of her too, but he had a hard time saying what. Maybe she was too tall. Maybe her smell was different. He tried to picture his mother's face but nothing came, nothing but a certainty that the woman he half saw beside him was all wrong. Was an imposter, wearing her memory like a crude, grisly costume. Suddenly the idea of her so close to him didn't give any sort of comfort at all.

Not his mother.

Wrong. All of it, wrong. *Wrong, wrong, wrong.*

The piano behind him let out a hollow chime.

He froze, the last book gripped in one trembling hand. He set it carefully on the shelf before slowly—very, very slowly—turning around.

A low, ugly sound crawled up his throat.

She sat on the hard wooden piano bench, her back rigid, fingers dangling over the ivory keys. Her hair might have been smooth or curled, but it was tangled and slick with gore, clumped into a clotted, soaking mess. Her posture stayed frozen as her head swiveled to find him. Her face was gone, unrecognizable, just two dark eyes above a ruined crater, pebbled in splintered bone. Broken ivory nubs poked out from a distended jaw. A sound echoed up from inside the wet, gruesome mess of her face, building, building, and then finally bursting forth.

"RUN!" the thing screamed in his mother's voice, and then she was standing, rushing toward him with arms outflung and he was falling, tumbling, catching himself on the bookshelf and scrambling through the gap. He dragged it shut behind him and then hurled himself up the stairs, sobbing as he fled into the dark, broken safety of the attic.

CHAPTER 3

THIRST drove him back down.

A day had passed—or was it more? Time had lost its anchor and the world blurred at the edges into a dream that wouldn't quite disperse. Daylight shifted into night and back again at least once, but beyond that Otto wasn't quite certain. The Orloj had tolled again and again, but the echoes seemed to ricochet meaninglessly across the city and get lost among the spires, waves tossing among themselves until the only thing remaining was an opaque, churning froth.

When he finally came to, the clouds above the window's narrow gaze held decadent streaks of soft candy pinks and oranges as the daylight surrendered and died. His mouth was packed full of sour, chalky grit and he tried to spit out the rancid taste, but couldn't manage the moisture. His stomach hurt, a hot acidic clench that reached up to his eyes, but the thought of choking down another dry cracker made him dizzy. His mind felt as bruised as his body, hazy and purple with vertigo.

He needed to drink, needed fresh water, and he needed it soon. The basest animal instinct. The first solid realization that had taken form in days.

The stockpiles of food his parents had hidden away in the attic were holding strong, but the stone jug of water had caught a bullet during the gunfire and lay in pieces. Dented tin drinking cups lay among the pile of broken dishes, but they were, of course, empty. Gathering water was one of his father's tasks, a job the man had performed without fail for nearly three years when he ventured down each night into the house below.

But the house below was home to something else now too. He'd heard them. The ghosts. As distant as the call of the Orloj but no less real. The occasional creak of footsteps through the empty halls, the murmur of voices and laughter. The sound of a voice—*her* voice—calling out his name again and again until he wanted to weep, yet lacked the tears.

Otto… Otto… Otto…

His throat gave a sticky click as he swallowed.

They might be waiting for him to step back into their domain, but he simply had no other choice, aside from lying down and accepting death. He had tried that for days now, and he could try no more. He had work yet to do. His father had told him that Death rang the bell at the great clock, and all the carved figures shook their head in refusal. Otto supposed he was no different.

Standing left him trembling and dizzy but he forced one cramped step after the next and down the attic stairs he went. It took him some time. Each unsteady pace became a dangerous proposition, and he leaned against the wall for balance.

When he could finally bring himself to slide it open—it made an awful, grinding grunt of a sound—the woman was gone. The library was empty.

Nothing waited to haunt him besides the boot prints smudging the floor and the faintest hint of lavender.

Had his mother smelled like lavender? Or was it *her*?

The smell was familiar, at least. A welcome reprieve from the stench of shit that clogged up the attic. He would need to empty the bucket they'd used as a toilet, he reminded himself. Grease the door. Gather food. Draw the water. Now that his parents were gone, it all fell on him. His mother, his father, reduced to the rituals they performed.

But first, the water.

He watched the room carefully for a minute longer, waiting to see if any apparition would coalesce, but nothing stirred. The piano in the corner kept its peace, undisturbed. No figure sat at it. No ghostly finger stroked its mechanical teeth. Otto pressed himself to the far side of the room as he crept by.

He peeked out from the library into the hallway he'd once roamed, back before the business of war began. His memories of the Before were blurry, muddled flickers, but seeing the relics of the life he once lived set them stirring in their graves.

The floral patterned hallway carpet where he would lay for hours during those final months, a reluctant captive flipping through books he couldn't yet read, waiting to head back out to the sun-drenched Letna or the riverbank.

It looks like rain, his mother would say when he asked. *Maybe we can go out tomorrow.*

Only it rarely did rain, and instead of listening to the soothing spatter of raindrops, Otto passed his time listening to the grumble of his father at work, his mother on the phone, and wishing for the sun on his face. The clang and click and heartbeat thrum of the clocks that crowded every corner of the house, and how they silenced, one by one, as his father took vital parts from them and carted the pieces through the library to his attic workshop. The sizzle of welding equipment he had borrowed from a local machine shop. The phone calls came more and more frequently, and his mother stopped pretending that the threat of weather was why she refused to let him leave the house.

He had been lying there on his back, half stupefied by the end of the wasted summer, when the call came in that sent them scurrying up to the attic while his father crouched, toolbox beside him, anchoring the bookshelf across the doorframe. He could remember the panic in his mother's voice, but not her words.

And not her face.

Boot prints trailed up and down the hallway. The doorways at either end opened up on empty bedrooms. A stairway directly across from the library led to the main floor. Between the library and his old bedroom, the dull last reaches of twilight crept in from the bathroom window and left a pale square upon the floor. Nothing stirred. No dead lady peeked out from the darkened doorways, no gurgling, ruined face peered up, half-hidden, from the shadowy caverns below the beds, his name on her blood-wetted lips.

He shuddered.

Water.

He shuffled down the hallway, his back to the wall until he reached the bathroom.

The sink did nothing when he twisted the handles, but the toilet was filled with dull, cloudy water and when he pried the porcelain lid off the toilet's tank, it was miraculously full as well. He thought he remembered his father saying the water there was clean, but as desperate as he was, he would have drunk the murk out of the bowl itself. Anything to ease the pounding ache in his belly and drive the taste of sour chalk out of his mouth. He cupped at the water with his hands at first, his fingers half numb from the chill, then simply buried his face in the tank when he couldn't claw it up to his cracked lips quickly enough. The porcelain pressed against his cheekbones as he gulped at the cold, sweet treasure, as it sloshed down his front and soaked his nightshirt in a frigid wave. He didn't stop until he was shuddering from relief as much as the cold. His stomach still hurt, but it was a different sort of pain and far more manageable.

Otto…

Otto spun around and pawed the wet from his face, eyes darting from the doorway to the tub. Empty. Just the wind somehow sneaking its way into the house, or the distant cry of the Orloj.

No faceless woman with a gruesome mask of ruined flesh, no man in black uniform with a fire burning inside him waiting and watching him in his moment of weakness. He clenched his hands together until the shaking slowed. He didn't dare try lifting the lid back onto the tank. Sound traveled through the house too easily, and he didn't want *her* to know.

Otto wondered briefly why the water still worked, but he supposed his parents must have figured that out. The mess of copper piping behind the toilet, maybe. One of his father's many inventions. A flip of the light switch confirmed that the electricity was out.

When he could hold himself steady again, he poked his head back out into the hallway. Still no ghosts. The gentle rush of wind sounded louder, distant snatches of voices and bustle, but all of that came from below and so he filed it away as unimportant. Maybe a window was cracked. He didn't dare venture all the way across to his parents' room—it stood to reason, in his mind, that if *she* was imitating his mother she might be hiding there in wait—but he had no need to. He could picture it clearly despite the years, the hulking wooden dresser with its carved feet, the clocks that nestled in the corners, the bed frame and thick mattress, even the way the light played in through the windows across the sheets at night.

Instead, he headed to his old room.

Some part of him brightened at the thought. His bedroom. He had been happier there, once, hadn't he? Back, years before? Flickers of his past reached out to him: the abstract menagerie of animal silhouettes that his mother had painstakingly stenciled along the top of the wall, the posters taped to the walls boasting a collection of motorcycles—Triumphs, Nortons, AJS bikes—that had once fascinated him in such a deeply elemental way. He realized he was grinning, for the first time in days.

But when he reached the room and looked inside, the smile vanished and he fought back tears, because the room was not his.

CHAPTER 4

IT had belonged to him once, he supposed, but the room had transformed. The walls seemed farther apart, yet the extravagance brought no comfort. The posters were peeling. The animal silhouettes looked like primitive cave paintings. The bizarre collection of shapes that crowded every surface, half-remembered, no longer provided the comfort they once had.

His father had packed the room with an assortment of inventions in various states of disrepair, designed out of curiosity as much as any real necessity. A rectangular metal speaker box, the face of it poked through with holes, was attached to a pipe that led into the floor, and Otto remembered his mother's voice booming up through it to tell him dinner was ready. A series of increasingly elaborate cuckoo clocks with loops of chain dangling from them like tails that were supposed to perform automated functions as time rolled by but had never been properly synched up, leaving Otto's bedroom in a constant stir of motion, of things emerging and vanishing and shifting.

The clocks were all dead. They had been gutted for parts, either fed into the metal man in the attic or into some other creation. Nothing ever stood long in the Braum household before it was tinkered with, upgraded, or broken and scrapped. His dad had been proud of that. *To each thing their time*, he'd insist. *If you're afraid to let go of the past it'll never let go of you.*

The city must have agreed, Otto guessed, because it had changed too. The houses outside the window were different than before. The roofs weren't brick red, they were the color of the stains on the attic floorboards. The white plaster faces of the buildings were shades of bone and tooth, of his father's eyes as he died. Maybe the whole world had transformed, maybe it was all one massive clockwork contraption in a constant state of cannibalistic change, grinding wheels and toothed cogs, gripping and pulling into upgrades or destruction.

He stepped as close to the window as he dared, looked down at the interlocking puzzle of cobblestones of the street below. The street was empty. Not like the last time he had looked down.

He heard the thunder of their feet before he saw them, felt the vibrations in the pit of his stomach. Boots stamping down on stone, a defiant, powerful sound that echoed through Otto's small chest and vibrated in his bones and he had pulled himself up against the window to look down the street for the source of the celebration. He didn't need to wait long.

First a few boys, boys not all that much older than Otto, running down the street in their tan uniforms and waving leaflets and flags as they hooted and howled and shouted out their excitement. Adults followed not long behind, faces peeked from windows, men and women leaked out onto the street to watch. The blast of trumpets swelled as people joined in the throng, as the footsteps grew louder. More and more flags waved, swung overhead by men and women, many that Otto recognized. Mr. Marek from down at the Havelska markets. Mrs. Vera from the ice cream parlor down off the Mala Strana. Even old Ms. Fena, the sharp-tongued lady next door who looked like Otto thought a person was supposed to look before they died of old age, stood out there, hunched and squinting with a banner clutched between her clawlike hands. Flags in red and white and sporting what looked like a peculiar black windmill.

And then it was no longer individuals, but a gathering, a single entity of bodies that marched on by in parade, and Otto felt himself beaming, his hands pressed together in excitement. Others were celebrating elsewhere, screaming with delight. Distant hollow pops sounded out from the storefronts. Men in gray marched, line by line, their legs straight and rigid in perfect, mechanically sweeping waves. The crowds parted around them, cheered them on. More hollow pops that the thunderous parade couldn't quite conceal. He hoped they were fireworks. He loved fireworks. They didn't sound right, though.

"What're those bangs?" Otto asked. His parents stood behind him, watched silently as he pressed his face to the smooth, chilly glass.

"A party," his mother said, but her voice was quiet. "A celebration. Judah?"

His father said nothing.

"Can I go down and see?" Otto asked.

"No," she whispered.

He almost started to whine, but then he saw the expression on her face and suddenly none of it seemed joyous at all. The shouts weren't delighted, they were furious. The stomping boots were a warning. Toothless old Ms. Fena was grinning, her mouth a night black slit as she looked up at him in the window. She held her banner higher.

His father jerked the curtain shut.

"Be careful of her, Otto. That one will hurt you."

The curtains had been opened since then, and Otto shrank back from the exposed window. If anyone on the street looked up and saw him... He thought of Ms. Fena. He wondered if she was still out there, waiting, her mouth an ugly, toothless pit and her shriveled eyes squinting for a glimpse of him.

The bed looked achingly soft compared to the stained mattress upstairs. For a moment he considered abandoning the attic entirely but he flinched at the thought, the guilt as heavy in his stomach as the weight of cold water. The attic mattress was his bed. He'd shared it with his parents for the last two and a half years. He could still feel their presence in the dents and dips. He wouldn't abandon it now. He wouldn't abandon it *ever*.

Besides, the ghost woman who had impersonated his mother was still roaming about somewhere, and there was no way to know if closing the door behind him would do any good at keeping her out. Maybe, he thought, she was the ghost of Ms. Fena. He shivered again.

His nose was running again, had been ever since he'd dunked his face into the cold water, and he wiped it on his sleeve. His shirt felt like it was made of ice. The attic was warmer. Drier. There were clothes up there, he reminded himself. Even the stench of waste seemed a comfort.

He shuffled back out and down the hallway, fully intending to head back up, but instead, on an impulse, he veered down the stairs toward the ground floor. He was halfway down before he realized the front door was still open.

Open.

The street beyond was calm. The sound of laughter reached him from far away. Families, chattering along as they wrapped up their day, finished their suppers, closed up shops, went for winter-kissed strolls, people content and completely oblivious to his world's apocalypse. As if none of it had ever existed.

As if the Braums had never mattered at all.

Somehow the dismissal was just as much of an abomination as the parades from before, maybe even more so. To hate was one thing, but to simply ignore the suffering of others was a strange and dreadful sort of evil.

They wouldn't ignore his presence if they saw him, though.

The stairwell was horribly exposed from the front door, and if anyone passed by while he climbed down…

His mouth felt dry again. The open space constricted around him, gripped his heart in a fist that cut each beat into a frantic flutter.

He needed to go down. He couldn't stay hidden away with the door wide open. Sooner or later, someone would come in. And if they came in, they'd inevitably come up. He didn't dare let himself think about the danger as he forced one foot down and then the next. Down he climbed.

The outside world peered in at him, the sprawling sky like the eye of some unfathomably massive and unendingly hostile giant. Twilight choked the blue into black, and distant stars flecked like shattered glass among the cataract clouds that expanded, that continued, that sprawled upward and outward into infinity.

Otto's breath came in choked, stuttering gasps at the sheer *openness* of it. Of the limitless expanse. Of the strange, cruel certainty of an idiot god looking down at him without pity or understanding.

He fought a momentary urge to flee, to run as fast as his legs would carry him out of the house that held only ghosts and pain, to sprint down the open road past storefronts and houses until he found himself back in the open fields where he'd once flown a kite. No one would notice him. They couldn't tell who he was... only he knew that somehow they would. Somehow, they'd all know, they'd all point to him and call out, and the faceless man in black with his burning cigarette would be waiting.

There was no hiding from the eyes of God. Wasn't that what the rabbis said? But all Otto could really think of was his father, his hair a mess and beard billowing with fingers pressing into Otto's collarbone to point him toward the attic window.

There are worse things than death, this father had assured him. *Look to the west and on a clear day you'll see the smoke. That's the train station to Chelmno.*

Otto never could see smoke. Sometimes he thought the sky got blurry out that way, but the attic window was angled too steeply. He wasn't even entirely sure what Chelmno was, but he could feel the distant thrum of trains heaving themselves along tracks from the factory centers, the delighted shrill of their steel wheels slicing against the rails. He could picture their furnaces, stocked full of screaming men, and blazing orange through slits like eyes. Hungry monsters, prowling on wheeled feet.

A man's voice reached him, humming an unfamiliar song as he ambled down the street. Otto was completely exposed, trapped on the stairwell. There was no going back up, so he scampered forward and hunched behind the door and waited. The steps came closer, closer… and then continued on by. He must have seen the open door, but he did not hesitate and check in, did not pause his humming, and it occurred to Otto that the open door might not be an unfamiliar sight. That countless other doors throughout the city might be left open, gutted, the residents no more than stains on the floorboards.

Otto waited until he could no longer hear the man's voice before he set his hands against the door.

He wondered if he'd ever see the outside world again. His parents wouldn't. There had been a time they last looked out and then never again and that seemed a crime. There was power in seeing the open sky, not through some greasy window, but with his naked eye. Even among the hateful infinity, there was something beautiful and awe-drenched in its pure, unrefined power.

The Orloj may have been the greatest work of man, but it held nothing on a glance at the sky.

He bit down against the inside of his cheek and pushed.

The door swung shut, clicked into place and Otto slid the bolt home.

CHAPTER 5

OTTO sank to the floor with his back against the door, his heart pounding, breath scarcely drawing. Some part of him wished he could hear a knock at the other side simply to know it was over, that the suspense was finished. That so much fear could be replaced by simple pain, pain that he could understand, pain that had to end the same way his parents' pain had ended. Pain that would be devoured by the trains as they consumed his body and breathed him out as smoke.

He pushed the thought away. No one was coming. No one had seen him. He was... safe? That wasn't the right word, but it was close enough. The house was his again.

He crept away from the front foyer, from the distant bustle of life, and was halfway up the stairs when he forced himself to stop.

He had come down from the attic for a purpose. Thirst was part of it, but he needed a solution to the inevitable problem of food, too. The front door was closed, the ghosts were asleep or at least absent for the moment. The dusk granted enough light to see by, but enough shadows that no one should notice him if he was careful. Now was the time to find what he needed.

Otto drew a slow, unsteady breath and then let it out.

He peeked his head inside the front study, but with the tall windows looking out into the street, he didn't risk entering. He considered checking the closet, but it was too near the front door. Instead, he headed down the hallway to the kitchen.

Somewhere inside, a perpetually nervous man from the synagogue used to drop off food. His father had never let him meet the man, but one time shortly before the phone call, Otto had crouched at the top of the stairwell, looking down, and listened to them converse. He was supposed to be asleep in his room, but he didn't yet understand the risks of getting caught. It was easy enough to see down into the foyer while remaining more or less invisible, if you kept your head low.

The two men were dressed in formal black long suits and kippahs, their beards spilling down across their chests, but aside from that they shared little. Otto's father was tall and hard-bodied, his posture proud and his voice a low rumble. The other man wiped the sweat from his palms on his wide frame. A large package was under one of the portly man's arms, wrapped in newspaper.

They spoke quietly and Otto didn't dare get too close, so he could only make out bits and pieces, fragments of names and places that didn't mean much to Otto. Names of streets. Names of towns. The names of men who Otto did not know. The two headed to the kitchen and rummaged around for several minutes. Otto considered sneaking back to his room, but then they reemerged, stood in the foyer in plain sight.

"Any time I can, I'll drop off more. Same place. But pace yourself, it might be a few days," the nervous man said. "If Heydrich is really coming…" He scratched at his bearded cheek and glanced up, almost directly at Otto, but his eyes passed over without stopping.

Otto's father had nodded, reached into the pocket of his jacket and held out a small bag held shut with a drawstring. "We'll make it work."

The man opened it, peeked inside, and then closed it. "You don't have to."

"Yes. We do," Otto's father said. "She won't be out there wearing jewelry anytime soon anyway."

The man had shaken his head. "I hope you're wrong," he said, but he didn't offer any disagreement. The bag rattled as he slipped it into his pocket.

After that there were no more meetings. The following day, the phone call. Then Otto's father summoned his mother and him up to the attic, and there they stayed.

But his father had still gone back down into the house, every night. Every night, he emptied the waste bucket and drew the water. Every night he roamed the rooms below. And, some nights—maybe once a week—he would return to the attic with a package of crackers, flatbread, sometimes salted meat or canned soup and vegetables, all wrapped in newspapers. Packs of candles, books of matches, batteries for the radio.

The news. Their food. Their light. All of it, hidden somewhere in the kitchen.

Without a window looking in, the kitchen was heavy with gloom, and Otto fumbled around in a drawer beside the entrance until he found a skinny stump of a candle, a thin cardboard matchbox lying beside it. The few remaining inside rattled like bones.

The shadows danced as he hefted the candle and tried not to think just how much the matchstick sulfur smelled like gun smoke. How the dark man's cigarette had glowed with that same captive fire.

The cabinets, the refrigerator that no longer hummed with life, the pans and spatulas hanging on the walls. The cutting board beside the empty knife block. The oven range, a massive propane-powered box that carried a hulking air of menace in its glossy white bulk. He remembered his mother being so proud of it, of the way it could ignite without a match or needing to be plugged in, some internal spur clicking over to strike a spark. One of the new models imported from… somewhere. Otto couldn't remember that part. It had been brand new when they went into hiding, his father nearly bouncing with delight as he poked around inside it to inspect what made it tick, but the years had weathered it despite the lack of use.

First Otto checked the pantry, but the shelves inside had been picked over. He climbed the ancient wooden stepladder to inspect the upper shelves, in case they'd been overlooked, but nothing remained besides a pair of boxes, lying on their sides, open mouths leading to empty shadows. Mouse droppings pebbled the shelves beside shaved bits of the cardboard that had been stripped off by years of rodent teeth.

He checked the cabinets, but the doors opened up on mostly empty sockets. A plate here, a bowl there. Two chipped coffee mugs and a teacup. More dark rice-shaped speckles, the only sign of life among the graveyard.

Otto left the cabinets open.

Nothing.

If there really were more than the crackers in his father's upstairs stash, Otto couldn't imagine where the stash had been hidden. If it was hidden anywhere at all. The nervous man had to know that his parents were dead. Otto had enough crackers in the bags upstairs to last a family of three for a few weeks, but after that...

And who knew? Maybe it was that nervous man who had turned them in.

Kill. Let them be erased.

He flexed his hands, fought back a shiver that had nothing to do with the chill.

"*Yimakh shemo*," he said. The words felt ugly in his mouth.

A flurry of sounds echoed in response, the scratching whisper of needle-thin claws on metal.

Otto spun to face the sound, his eyes roving over the countertops, the open cabinets, the oven range. The candle guttered and danced, the shadows shifted, but nothing else stirred.

The scratching continued.

Something was in the kitchen with him. Something moving, but invisible.

Something alive.

He choked down the burst of panic. Mice, he realized. It had to be mice. He'd seen the droppings. The clicking and skittering were simply mice tumbling about inside the guts of his mother's stove, tiny living sounds magnified by the hollow metal box, disturbed by the voice of an intruder so close by after months of silence.

A seething, furious loathing boiled up in Otto's gut.

Mice. Living in his home. In his *home*. They'd moved in and made their claim and it didn't matter one bit that his parents were dead, not to them, they were all too happy to take, take, take. To move in. To steal his food. To leave their filthy little pellets along the floors his mother used to sweep. To scare him when he was all alone.

They'd taken his food, he bet. Shredded the newspaper, gobbled it all up and left nothing for him.

Kill

He flipped the oven dial on and pressed the igniter spur. The beast let out a low hiss of gas and a dull *THWUMP* as the flame lit.

The fire would scare them off, would drive them back wherever they came from, and maybe then they'd think twice before invading his house. Otto bared his teeth as the hot breath spilled out in a wave across his legs. He waited to hear their tiny feet scamper away from the unbearable heat…

But they didn't.

The temperature climbed.

Instead of scampering, he heard an awful sound—horrible, squeaking screams. A helpless animal panic that echoed inside of the empty metal box and could almost have sounded human.

The tattered cardboard. What if they were making a nest?

They were burning inside, he realized. Burning alive. The babies too, a family screaming in helpless panic as they incinerated.

Otto turned the stove off, wrenched open the door, and the smell hit him like an open-handed slap.

Burnt hair. Burnt meat.

What waited inside was a nightmare of small, melted body parts fused to the stove's flooring, eyes clouded and baked blind, bared yellow teeth at odds with the scorched hairless flesh. Bony feet cracked like clay. They must have huddled together as they roasted. They must have clung to each other in their final moments, moments that hadn't yet run out because they keened and screamed inside their prison, cried out to him like he was some terrible, negligent god in their world. He'd let them burn. Worse than that. He'd lit the fire.

Otto slammed the door shut—part of him noting that the crash of metal on metal was loud, far too loud, that someone could hear and notice—and he groped around on the countertop until he found a spatula.

His hands shook as he gripped the oven door and heaved it open, a vague idea of trying to save the mice, to save even one, maybe just to offer some pitiful gesture of comfort to the gruesome mess… but the oven was empty.

Nothing.

No bodies. No whiplike tails sizzling as they smoldered like lit cigarettes, like the trails behind red-spangled kites.

Nothing at all.

The stove looked different, strange in a way that hurt to think about, set his head pounding and vertigo flooding in from the corners of his vision. He thought he was going to be sick. He eased the oven door back shut, stepped away from it, edged toward the ransacked pantry.

Thump-thump-thump

At first he thought it was a fist pounding on the front door, but far worse—the sound of footsteps. Footsteps, tumbling down the stairs and closing in on him. Fast.

From the foyer a voice called out.

Otto? Is that you?

"Please. Go away," Otto whispered, but his voice was all wrong somehow, too.

Weaker, rougher, cracked with age. Not just creaking from disuse, either. *Old.* Ancient. Like those wrinkled, weathered men at the synagogue, their beards in dull, unhealthy grays and their voices creased with the rasp of aged leather. Otto could never focus fully on their words, instead spent his attention hoping the men would take deep drinks of water to clear their throats. The candle's flame trembled as Otto inspected the liver spots climbing his withered, scabby arms like strange ivy, the mottled silver scars that sliced cruel paths up his wrists beneath the thin-wired shroud of colorless hair.

Old?

He blinked and his arms were back to their proper selves again. There was no time to think about it, no point in guessing what strange trick the candle's glow had played. The footsteps had almost reached the kitchen. He snuffed the light out and stumbled backward, pulled the pantry shut behind him. He huddled back against the shelving, squeezed his eyes shut as tight as he could. Tiny, terrified sounds clawed and scrabbled up his throat but he swallowed them down, choked them into submission, forced them back inside. He thought of the mice, melted by the blasting heat.

Otto? the voice called out again, a cruel play at kindness. Not from the front hall, but from the kitchen. The wicked smile in her voice set a ripple across his skin, weakened his bladder. *Ottoooo…*

The footsteps came closer, closer, closer. Paused just outside the pantry.

He'd wakened the ghosts when he slammed the oven door. He'd disturbed them and now they were searching for him. Now *the woman* was coming to hurt him.

Ilsa.

The name came to him from nowhere, popped into his head without any prompting, nearly slipped from his mouth, but he squeezed the spatula as tightly as he could, pursed his lips together and waited, swore to himself he would never again leave the attic if he somehow escaped undetected. The lack of water, the poisonous stench of the bucket, all of that could find some other solution on a different day. One more chance, that's all he needed. One more chance.

Then the footsteps began to move again, through the kitchen, out into the hall and away. When the sound was far enough, he did not wait.

He fled.

CHAPTER 6

T HE following night, Otto broke his promise. He didn't yet need to go back down, but he went anyway. He did again the night after, and the night after that, and that quickly it became a habit, just as it had for his father before him.

He wasn't sure why he risked it. He had his reasonings and justifications, but they were nakedly false. Each evening when he slipped back up to the hard, unforgiving mattress where his parents had once slept, he promised himself he would stop. Each day when he woke up, he promised himself that this night would be different. That the cups he filled with water could sustain him, that the bucket had been emptied and wouldn't fill up for days. This night, he'd stay. And as the day turned toward dusk and the Orloj called out and the stains on the floor grew dark, he made himself a liar again and again.

Anything was better than staying.

So down the stairs he crept, slipped through the bookcase door and into the library below to wait breathlessly for the sound of her shuffling footsteps, to listen for the hollow voice calling out his name—*Otto? Otto, is that you? Otto, where are you?*—that would set him scurrying back up to safety.

Some evenings he found she had been in the library, had rearranged books or turned the bench. Some mornings he even woke to the echo of hollow piano notes seeping up through the attic door, but by the end of the day it was always still once more and he would poke his head around the corner, watch the empty room with careful survivor's eyes before testing the floorboards for creaks that might summon her. If he was quiet, if he was very quiet, she seldom came searching and only rarely did he find himself slipping up behind doors or slithering under furniture to wait for her to shuffle on by. He wasn't sure why the silence helped. Maybe, he guessed, it was because she had no eyes. He certainly didn't know why she hadn't been able to follow him that first time, back up the stairs, did not know what would happen to him if she caught him straying from the safety of above, but he didn't dare risk it.

He avoided his parents' bedroom, just the same.

While the daylight held sway, it was her time, and he stayed hidden in the attic. But after dark, so long as he was careful, she was nothing more than a distant murmur and he could drift like a ghost himself through the empty house, attending to the basic necessities of life. He practiced lifting the tank lid from the toilet and setting it silently back in place, the cups full of water by his feet. He got used to pouring his waste into the toilet and fleeing before the bowl had fully cleared itself. He wiped half-heartedly under his arms with a cold wash cloth, dipped in the water, the way his mother used to.

He knew he should change his clothes, but there was some comfort in the filthy blue pajamas he had worn on that terrible night, so instead of rummaging through the laundry that the soldiers had left in a stomped heap, he simply set the rough weight of his father's workshop smock on over top. It hung down to his knees, so he strapped the brown leather toolbelt around his waist. When he snuck back down to the kitchen to check again for food and the tiny, furry shapes darted by, he no longer felt anger or fear, but a kind of grudging kinship as he watched their furtive, nervous scampering.

Then he started looking for jobs to do.

What, exactly, wasn't all that important. He needed the tasks more than the tasks needed doing. Time seemed both precious and decidedly dull, the weeks passing in a blur while the days dragged on interminably. He supposed life had been monotonous before too, but he had his parents, had his toys, had his lessons and schedules and classes, first scribbled on paper and later with a chalk on a slate board. He had a routine and he had been accustomed to it. Now… he thought of his mother's constant cleaning, painting, reorganizing, how she had moved their few pieces of furniture to new places within the limited space, frowning with concentration as if it were a vital task. His father's prayers, his endless toiling on the metal man. Maybe he had never finished building the golem because he feared what would be left, once his mission was completed. Maybe a lot of life was like that.

And so, Otto greased the joints and track of the hidden library door until it eased open and closed without so much as a creak. He checked the windows to make sure they were safe and sealed. He roamed until he sensed night was coming to a close, the first birds chirruping and the distant rolling thunder of planes and cars and stirring voices outside, and then he retreated back upstairs and reality seemed to unpick itself at the seams. He counted time by the shifting shadows and the call of the Orloj.

Sometimes he wondered if he was really there at all when the sunlight crept in and lit the attic with its dull glow, or if it was illuminating an empty room. He slept strange hours, often woke to find himself nestled against the great metal man his father had built instead of on the mattress. The golem had done nothing to protect him, but it had made a fist at their death, and the simple gesture—that recognition of outrage—was all he had. A pittance, and a profusion.

Otto slept as much as he could during the daylit hours, dozed through the hazy, late-winter glow until darkness returned. He tried to read, since the light permitted it without wasting any of his sparse supply of candles, but never for very long. Reading was hard. His mother had taught him, but without her there it all seemed an overwhelming task. Besides, there wasn't much that interested him. He didn't want to read her cookbook, because it made his stomach hurt. The Torah made his heart hurt. The journal his father kept while building his creations was the least offensive, but the hand-writing was cramped and confusing and dense with scrawled notes, the blotted ink like bloodstains. Time itself seemed distorted, would stretch and shrink to match his father's handwriting. His back ached from lying down, but he was afraid to pace. He waited and waited, day after day, until at last the shadows grew longer and he seemed to solidify. His mind finally found its anchor among the confused waters, and then he was ready to start again.

By the end of the first week, when he couldn't find anything worth doing, Otto began to gather supplies. Room by room he wandered, examining cabinets and countertops and furniture and running his hands across the pitiful items that remained. Some, he took back to the attic whole. Some, he only took pieces. Others, he left alone. The only room that was spared was his parents' old bedroom, in case he might find the woman sleeping there.

He wasn't sure how he knew which to gather. He wasn't even sure what the items signified, or why he harvested them. The table legs from the kitchen table were carefully unscrewed from their moor-ings and migrated with him, but not the table top. Kitchen utensils came—two at a time so that he did not risk them rattling—but not the cups or bowls. The old wooden stepladder from the pantry came, whole. The seat from a stool in the front closet. The mattresses from the rooms stayed despite the warmth they might have offered. When he visited his old bedroom, he carefully unscrewed and removed the speaker box and the metal length of piping that his father had installed, leaving in its place a hole in the floor leading directly down into the kitchen. He snuck from room to room, eyes roaming, the pockets of his smock overfull, only slinking back up to the attic when his shoulders ached from the load.

He gathered springs and tiles, wood and metal, cloth and nails and screws. All the tiny scraps he could fit in his pockets, picking the house clean of everything useful. Some evenings, he found himself wondering if it was his home at all, or if the attic somehow opened up to a different world that changed by the day, where he could enter the same room and find it a separate place from the day before. Always some fresh discovery, some new thing to be harvested.

The only rule he knew for sure was that They needed to not catch him. Whether "They" meant the dead woman or Ms. Fena or the dark man or a spare glance through the window from the soldiers who patrolled the streets outside seemed to vary night by night, but if anyone caught him, it would be over. Of that he had no doubt. At the first sign of footsteps, the first call of his name, he darted back to safety above, his body clammy with sweat and heart stampeding in his chest.

He piled his gatherings in a heap, up there, among the tattered and broken bits that the awful men left behind. The first reaches of spring shook off the grip of winter. The nights crept by and the pile grew as his supply of crackers dwindled, first by half, then by half again. He started rationing. The stains on the floor faded until he could sometimes convince himself they were some splash of brown from decades gone by, although other days they seemed fresh and glossy and they left him weeping with how badly he hurt from the wanting. For food. For comfort. For love.

Then one day, when he woke up, he knew in his heart what he had been gathering and why.

He set to work.

CHAPTER 7

"**T**HAT thing is an abomination."

"It's a tool, Ruth."

"You're playing God."

The man shrugged. "Does that matter? God isn't going to stop them."

"Of course it matters. It's a hateful thing. It's made for killing. The world has enough killing."

Oily rags layered between stacks of metal plates and bolts made bookends to their mattress, crowded in every bit of free space. His father's welding equipment was no longer upstairs, but he had a small hand-cranked drill that he worked tirelessly, punching holes so that he could feed screws through.

"When those bastards come knocking down our door, it won't matter."

"It always matters," his mother said. Then she cocked her head toward Otto, "and they're not going to knock down our door, little lamb."

Otto nodded dutifully along. He was bored and confused and wasn't sure why he wasn't able to play in his room. A week ago, his father had invited the two of them up to the attic, showed them what he'd spent the last month working on. Just in case of emergencies, he told them. Preparation was a blessing.

The attic had been transformed. No longer was it some creepy, cobwebby realm of a workshop and that one storage chest that showed up in Otto's nightmares for reasons he couldn't quite understand. The ceiling was still a high, angled peak way up among the rafters, but the floor had wooden boards across it and furniture had been set in place, separated into rooms by clean curtain dividers.

Otto's dad had walked them around the perimeter, pointing out each and every thing he could—the storage chest now packed with dry, unappealing food and candles and matches, clothes in drawers, plates and bowls and silverware all neatly stacked, even a bucket that was somehow supposed to be an emergency toilet, which caused Otto to giggle before he realized his dad was serious—before finally arriving at The Thing.

The one item he had avoided mentioning.

The metal man.

The memory was one of the earliest Otto could still hold clearly in his mind. He remembered bits and pieces of his life in the house below, but mostly in the way he could remember the words to a song when he heard the music. None of it existed without cues to anchor it together, and the memories themselves only consisted of short snippets, blurred conversations and emotions that he sometimes doubted. He sometimes wondered if the world before the attic was something he'd really experienced, or just something pieced together from his imagination, the same as the stories he used to act out with the blocky wooden toys that now hung, magicless and dead in the bag on the wall.

The golem wasn't complete, of course, back then. When Otto first saw it, it'd been little more than a frame and a pile of scrap metal, cogs, gears and wire, its future design no more than skeletal notes on pages that poked out from the brown leather beast that was his father's journal. The journal was packed half full of diagrams, notes and planned contraptions, and it accompanied him everywhere. Every new creation got painstakingly filed within it, and Otto thought of the book as something nearly living, as much a sibling as a collection of notes. Even when his father's inventions didn't work—and they failed about as often as they worked—Otto clapped and cheered each one's completion and his dad would smile behind his bushy beard, ruffle his son's hair and pat the book. Otto's mom would just shake her head and smile, her face glowing with pride. Until the golem.

That thing is an abomination.

If so, it was a broken one.

It had fallen face down to the floor, bent at the waist, and the entire internal structure had been knocked out of alignment. Otto tried to heave it upright, but the thing was simply too heavy for him to move and the outer shell was dented, punctuated with bullet holes, and bent so far that it could not sustain the weight even if he could get it back into position. Not all together, then. In parts.

The bottom half of the man appeared mostly undamaged, so first Otto unbolted the broken portions and dragged them aside, and then he set about peeling off the metal frame that still remained attached. He sorted through his father's toolbox until he found the crowbar, planted it in the crack in the mangled torso plate and flung his scrawny weight against it until his hands ached and his knobby arms trembled. He nearly gave up, but then the bar began to pivot and he stumbled, off-balance as the plate slid free and crashed against the ground. He waited after that, terrified that someone might have heard—was old Ms. Fena still next door? Could the faceless woman have heard? Was the dark man still smoking, smiling from the shadows?—but no one came and his fear faded not long after the echoes.

His wiped greasy jelly from his fingers on his father's apron as he peered into the guts of the thing. Gears and cogs, hollow gaps, bars and belts. He wasn't altogether sure what was necessary or not, but since the golem had failed to awaken in its moment of need, Otto supposed maybe that didn't particularly matter. He wasn't going to manage pure replication. He didn't have his father's skill and vision, nor did he have years to plan. He simply had the journal and hand tools and scraps, so he worked as best he could, plucking piece after piece from the broken body and transferring it over and bolting it into place on the undamaged base. The welding wasn't an option, but there were screws to spare and the internal pieces seemed designed to all grip each other. The portions he could not salvage, he replaced with bits harvested from furniture and filed to fit. When one gear turned, he could see others shifting through a hole in its side, metal prongs biting against others like the fingers of interlocking hands.

"*The trick,*" *his father confided,* "*is hidden in ancient stories, passed down from father to son for generations. No one wrote it down. No one dared. Too much chance of it falling into the wrong hands. A thing like this can change the world.*"

Otto nodded. Otto's mother watched on with disapproval, but she had stopped protesting it as much now that they had lived in the attic for the better part of a year.

"*What's the trick?*"

Otto's father simply shook his head. The journal was wedged open in front of him, loose pages carpeting the floor. Each scrap of paper was covered in symbols, in letters and cramped scrawling along the borders, all fighting for space. He copied laboriously and seemingly at random from the pages onto the gears as he worked.

"*Building isn't enough. It has to come with sacrifice. I write on each piece. Each word touches other words, each letter spells out a secret. You write them and fit them into place, and when you're done you write the word* emét *up on its forehead.*" *He tapped the journal.* "*And then... if you've given enough to it, it comes to life and does whatever you tell it to.*"

"*What's* emét?"

"*It means truth,*" *Otto's mother answered.* "*And if you erase the first letter, the aleph, it becomes death. You erase the first letter and the golem dies. That's what all the stories say. That's the important part.*"

Otto's father nodded. "*If you want it to die, yes.*"

"*It needs to die,*" *his mother said.* "*You have to promise me that you'll kill it when this is all through. That thing is hateful.*"

His father made a gesture with his head that might've been agreement, but he didn't say anything.

"And what's the secret?" Otto asked. "The one you're writing."

"The names of God."

Otto rummaged around in the pile he'd gathered, picked through the heap of dismantled furniture and scraps, until he found the pieces he wanted.

The back half of the torso was made of layered plates fixed to twin framing rods and after the better part of an hour he managed to slide them out from the wreckage. Mounting the rods to the trunk took another hour, but it allowed him to build higher. The back plates that Otto could manage to lift, he fixed back into place. Others stayed on the floor. The chest was still wide open, but that suited Otto well enough. He leaned through the opening to set gear after gear into place. Nothing matched quite perfectly. Too much damage had been done. Otto filled in the gaps from the scrap pile. The writing was jumbled into senselessness, but it would have to do. Each new piece he added, he scribbled a word, a letter, a name.

He ate from the stockpile of crackers and canned goods while he worked, his hands filthy with a thin, slick yellow oil. Everything he touched tasted vaguely burnt. Scrapes marked his arms in red lines that seemed, strangely, familiar. For the first time since that awful night, when he slept, he did not dream. His body ached when he woke, long after midday. He was still groggy and clumsy and fumbling when he started up again.

At night, he emptied the waste bucket into the toilet, the bowl gurgling quietly as the pressure caused it to drain itself. He filled his water cup from the tank. He ate from the dry stacks of crackers. He finished off the last can of green beans, cold; drank it straight from the sharp-edged can and afterwards gulped down the thick, tinted water in which the slimy things floated.

And then he returned to his mission. He no longer felt an urge to explore.

By the third evening, the torso had taken clear visual form.

Reattaching the arms would be a delicate task, but they had few damages themselves, so it would mostly be transfer work once he had the chest and shoulders completed. But there were other, more pressing concerns. The head remained in two pieces on the ground, the front mask that made the face all bent and bullet-holed, and Otto had no way to solder or weld it back into smoothness. The gap in the chest, where he had hidden, was no longer an option. The golem was not nearly as sturdy as before and the structure needed every bit of support that he could manage.

It took him a while to decide what to use, and how. The hand drill helped poke holes through the metal plates and let him set up anchoring points. He'd seen his father do it countless times, but working the drill's crank was far harder than it had seemed and his hands throbbed afterwards. He picked through the bent metal, the scraps and wreckage he had gathered, until his eyes came to rest on it: the broken lamp. His parents had kept it without having the electricity to turn it on, so it must have meant something to them. The porcelain base had taken a bullet, but the painted wooden curve of the body was largely intact and even the bulb remained. First, he bolted one of his toy knights against the metal framing rods as a brace. He set the broken lamp base against it, wedged the frame between the head and the body of the makeshift wooden horse and tightened the head of the toy until it became a vise. Then he bolted the metal neck of the lamp into place, toothy gears framing the bulb on every side.

It looked better, there. No longer just a broken scrap, now it was once more part of something. Now it had purpose. Across the polished face of the ceramic, he scraped the names of his mother and his father: Ruth and Judah. He didn't like how that looked so beneath it

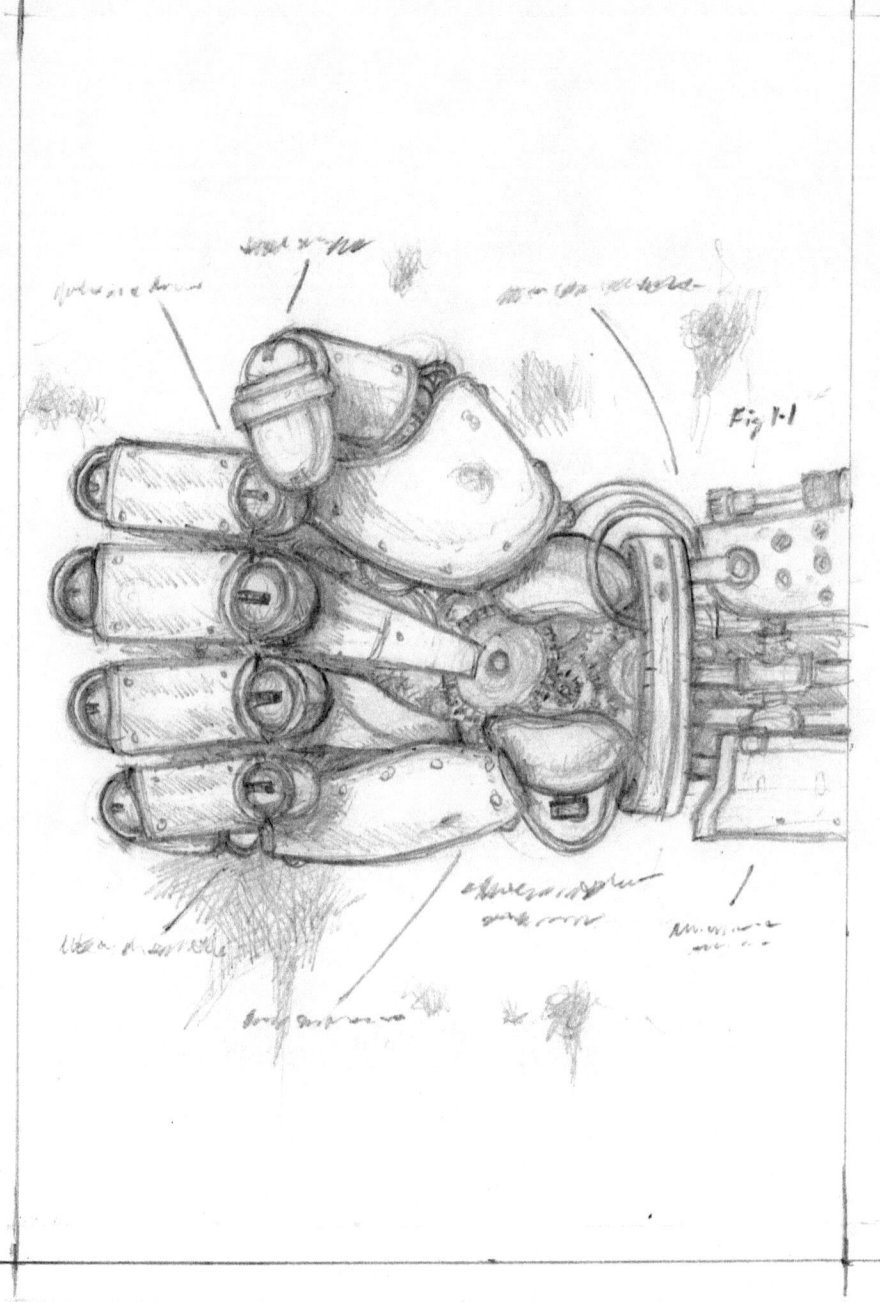

Fig 1-1

he etched in their real names: Mama. Papa. The dowel trembled in his hands when he was done, and he tried his best to not cry.

Not the names of God, but the next best thing.

He wished they were there with him. Wished more than anything to hear their voices. To have his mother wrap her arms around him. To have his father call out his approval at what he'd built. To chastise him for touching the tool chest. To hear either of them say anything at all.

But, like so many other inventions, the golem had failed them in their hour of need. Otto was left with a steel fist instead of his parents. When he eventually finished, what then? No more food was coming. There was no help on the way. The golem couldn't provide. A heap of junk, his mother had called it, and she was right. His memory of the kite, the tug of wind and the open sky made the effort all seem so hopeless and primitive.

He was half dozing, caught in his thoughts as the sunlight turned sallow, when noises from out front shook him from his reverie. The slam of car doors. Voices. Not moving along, either. He tried to remember if he'd made any mistake, any loud sound in the last day or so, but the panic blossoming up inside him muted his ability to remember much, choked out all rational thought in its poisonous vines.

They were coming. They were coming and the golem was nowhere near complete. The shoulder anchors were set, but without the plating and the arms attached they wouldn't do much good. The head still lay in two pieces on the floor. He thought of trying to hide inside the golem, but the gap he had used before was filled and even if he could still fit, he doubted it would do much good. Surviving before had been as much a matter of luck as any planning.

"They're leaving," Otto whispered to himself. "They're going to go."

He almost managed to believe, but he had spent so much time acclimating to the house that he felt the sliding of the deadbolt as much as heard it. The rattle of the doorknob shook away his denial. A thump. Voices, muffled, calling out. He pressed a palm across his mouth and held his breath.

The front door swung open.

CHAPTER 8

THE front door was open.

Open.

He was sure of it. The voices below echoed up, clearer than before. The distant, subtle sound of the street filtered in.

He sucked at air, but the breaths seemed to never quite reach his lungs, seemed to spill back out without surrendering their nourishment, tides against an unyielding beach. Each hammer blow of his heartbeat was more than a sound, screamed out in sentient language: *Open. Open. Open.*

The word blared through his mind again and again, a red-drenched siren that stained his thoughts and squeezed itself out of his skin in a slick of greasy sweat. He had closed it and locked it. He squeezed his eyes shut and remembered that day, his back to the wall, the click of the bolt sliding into place. He *had* locked it. No one could just open the door.

Unless they had a key. A key stolen, or a key made.

That meant they came with purpose.

The man in the black uniform, coming back to check out his handiwork. To make sure Otto and his family were still dead. One look at how much Otto had cleaned up would tell him everything he needed to know.

Otto scrambled up as close to the window as he could, but the slats kept him from seeing anything below.

Hiding wouldn't help him this time. If the man in black was there hunting him, nothing would.

He turned to look down the barrel of the stairwell.

Too early, a voice inside him whimpered. *The sun.*

He shuddered. Sunlight was *her* time.

Someone was speaking down in the front foyer. The words were indecipherable, but the sound was undeniable. He had to know, he realized. He could do it, too. He'd spent all those hours slinking from shadowy room to shadowy room, darting in and out of closets and behind furniture. If he was careful...

He licked dry lips, his foot quivering as he climbed down the first step, then the second. A gray fog of all-enveloping terror spilled through his thoughts with each stammering beat of his heart, bursts of smoke from some strange internal, infernal engine.

Then he was at the bottom. He forced his body to move, to simply move and not to think. It took him three tries to grip the brass handle firmly enough to work the bolt and slide the bookcase on its track.

The room was empty. Still. No hideous phantom crouched over the piano, dripping fresh blood on the ivory keys and peering up from beneath a screen of knotted, gore-snarled hair. No crooked fingernail reaching out toward the vulnerable skin below his neckline. No rancid, rotting breath rasping out his name.

She was gone. *For now,* he reminded himself.

She probably knew how to hide just as well as he did.

The intruders were speaking again, far more clearly. German. He crept out from the library on his hands and knees—*hallway clear*—and toward the front stairwell vantage point where he had once crouched to watch his father meet the man who brought them groceries.

The door was indeed open. Sunlight streamed in and carried with it a breath of cold air.

A leathery suitcase stood beside the door and then a girl walked in and set a second valise beside it. Otto shrank back, expecting her to be faceless too, but she was just a girl in a drab green dress. Maybe eleven or twelve, eyes bright and blue, wide-lipped and skinny and distracted with excitement.

A woman entered a minute later to stand beside the Girl.

She wore a glaringly red hat with a brim and a belted tan over-coat, and the first thing she did was to touch the table in the entryway, as if to read how much of her weight it could support. Not that it would need to support much. She was rail thin and while she looked like she had once been achingly pretty, she now mostly looked tired. The Woman.

"Birgitte," she called out. Other words in German, spoken too quickly for Otto to understand.

The Girl followed her across the front foyer and toward the kitchen. To see them there, he'd need to move and he didn't dare risk it.

Over the years, men would periodically check the house below, but their visits were always brief and purposeful and the voices that leaked up through the floorboards never belonged to women. Let alone a twelve-year-old girl.

These weren't secret police come to drag him out from his hole and send him off to join that distant horizon smudge. They were a family. His head ached. The sunlight streaming in was too much, too bright, and none of it made a bit of sense.

"Go away," he whispered, mouthed the words so quietly that he himself could barely hear them. In his mind, he shouted it out, again and again. *Go away!*

A third voice boomed out.

The Woman called him Frank, but to Otto he was simply the Man. He stood tall, taller than Otto's father by a full head, and wider shouldered too. His height hid his face as he closed the door behind him. Otto only caught a glimpse of the bottom half of the Man's face as he set his two suitcases alongside the Woman's and the Girl's. His mouth made a thin, unsmiling line.

The two rushed back to meet him, grabbed him by either hand and yammered away at each other, crowing out their delight at each new discovery, babbling sounds of confusion and laughter at the disassembled tables and chairs.

They spread out, their footfalls and ugly yammering drawing a map of the first floor as they explored. As they examined all the things that Otto's family had once owned. And Otto listened, his mind staggered with disbelief.

Upstairs would be next, he realized. And they were moving quickly.

He slid himself away from the banister on his belly and scurried, low to the ground, back into the library. He was easing the bookcase doorway back into place as they mounted the stairs. A moment after he slid the lock into place, they came spilling into the room.

He froze in place. He didn't dare climb higher up the stairs, didn't dare so much as draw a deep breath as the others spoke on the far side of the wall. A creak could betray him. He prayed they couldn't hear the thunder of his heart.

Their words tangled together in their excitement, climbing over each other in an ivy of hard consonants. Otto could only understand bits and pieces. He had learned enough German to speak the parts that mattered, but few of the complexities, and their accent made it hard for him to untangle. The words he could recognize pounded the terror home, sharp pointed stakes driving into the rocky soil of his heart.

Words like *room* and *school*.

The Woman spoke more clearly than the Man, and when she at last repeated the first word the Man had said, Otto finally understood it.

Home.

They weren't here to find him. They weren't casually looking around. The Woman. The Girl. The suitcases.

His lower lip trembled. Not fair. It didn't belong to them. The voices faded out of the library and a small sob escaped him.

Home.

A rustling sounded only a matter of feet away. The Man called out and the Girl answered, not from the hallway, but from the library. From the far side of the bookshelf itself. Had she heard him?

There was nothing but the feeble doorway of plaster and wood and paper to separate them, and all at once the hatred and anger couldn't sustain him any longer and he was a child, just a kid, and he was so scared that it hurt. The nightmare wouldn't end. The only ones left to hear him cry out were the monsters themselves.

He clamped a fist across his mouth, pressed it against the bone beneath his nose until his vision blurred from the bruising pain. He imagined his fist like the great steel man's hand above.

For a moment he thought that she hesitated, but then she slid one of the few remaining books back into the shelf and headed out to join the others.

Home.

No, they weren't just visiting. He should have known that from the start. They were here to stay.

CHAPTER 9

OTTO watched the dying of the light from his mattress, staring up through the dirty window as the blue, and his thoughts, gave way to black.

The fear had receded a bit, and with the stranglehold loosened he could consider his situation a bit more clearly. He was trapped, sure, but he wasn't caught. He might not have another chance, once the morning came. Now was his time to pay them back. He wasn't sure what he planned—what to do or how to do it—but that didn't matter. He had to do *something*. They had come into his house and tried to claim it, after all. There was nowhere he could go. The metal man slouched beside him, the detached fist still clenched.

When the grimy window was fully dark and his eyes had adjusted to the gloom, Otto crept on shoeless, stockinged feet down the stairwell, careful to stay to the sides of each step in case it might creak. There he huddled up against the bookcase door, listening. Only silence. He waited a while longer anyway, jittery and trembling in the dark, until his stomach ached from hunger. He could have gone up, nibbled on the remaining scraps, but he knew that if he climbed up the stairs there was no way he would gather the momentum to come back down. He slid the bolt, let it click out of place and then eased the bookcase open. It glided smoothly, without a sound. He'd remembered to grease it. His father would be proud.

Would have been.

His lower lip trembled and he held onto the anger to keep his panic from stampeding out of control. *They* killed his parents. *They* stole his home. It was his time to be the man.

The ghost was absent, if she even survived the new intrusion. It was too deep of night for anyone else but him. *And the mice*, he thought, and bared his teeth at the dark. The library was smothered in shadow, colors choked into monotone. For a dizzying moment, he could barely recognize the room despite having snuck down night after night before. Everything looked slightly different, somehow. Was the piano sitting in a different corner? Was the rug shifted off center and somehow brighter and unstained by boots? But then it was all back to the correct way, and of course it was because they hadn't had time to change a thing.

He tried not to think about it, filed it away with the ghosts and his vanishing scars and the ache of his bones. And Ilsa.

Like a ghost himself, he drifted through the room and out into the hallway.

The house lay in stillness. The night sky trickled in from the windows and his vision swam with the thunder of his heartbeat. He prayed they couldn't hear it.

Step after step, his feet padded gently against the ground. A floorboard's creak froze him in his tracks, and he pressed himself, trembling, against the wall. He waited for a voice to call out his name, but no, it was still. The grumble of snores made their way down the hall. He took a deep breath in, held it until his lungs ached, and shoved it out through clenched teeth.

He wasn't going to hide. He wasn't going to let *Them* take his home while he cowered in the dark.

He wasn't sure what he planned to do, only that he needed to see *Them* there, to see *Them* sleeping and to know they were real and not more phantoms come to torment him. He set one finger against their bedroom door and guided it gently, ever so gently, open. Moonlight spilled in through the curtainless window and flooded the room.

The clocks and dressers made strange, humanoid silhouettes. Suitcases slumped, open, next to the dressers, their contents emptied. They'd already unpacked. How seamlessly his parents had been replaced. It felt obscene. Killing left an empty pit. Replacement was erasure.

Otto glanced at the twin lumps in the bed—for a moment, it seemed like there was only one—but they didn't stir as he stepped into the room. A lamp stood on the dresser next to a stained vanity mirror whose glossy darkness reminded Otto of the painted black eyes of his toys. And there, beside it, the knife. He drifted closer.

Not a knife like Otto had seen before. The handle was dull black wood, swollen nearly into a ball in the middle and oddly comfortable in his hand, despite the weight. A steel eagle had been stamped into the handle, the ugly windmill symbol in its talon grip, and something like two lightning bolts were set in near the metal pommel. The blade slid silently from its sheath. Sleek, double-edged, longer than Otto's hand and tapered to a wicked point. There was flowery script written along the blade but they weren't words that Otto recognized, and the weapon seemed more designed for function than ceremony.

It made Otto think of a tooth. A weapon. A tool for killing.

He wiped his hands on his pants, one by one, before turning to the sleeping shapes. The naked blade glinted in the moonlight. Across the room he crept. His heart thundered in his chest. Closer. He forced one foot in front of the next, the knife squeezed in his fist.

They're going to wake up! They're going to see you! They're going to scream!

He fought the internal voice down. Vertigo surged through him, threatened to send him spilling to the ground as the floor bucked under him. His hand seemed old one moment and young the next, shifting with each unsteady clench of his heart. Tears trickled down his face, unchecked.

Then he was at the bedside.

He hadn't fully appreciated just how big the man was. How small the weapon felt. How small *he* felt. The man cleared his throat in his sleep and Otto froze.

If he wakes up, you have to kill him.

Even if he didn't wake up, Otto should do it anyway. Someone had to die. There could be no other outcome. They were lying in the bed his parents had shared, in the home they'd cherished. They had come to stay and the old and the new couldn't coexist forever. Sooner or later, one had to replace the other. Sooner or later, one had to die. It was written in that train station smoke, in the stained floor of the attic, in the ugly branding on the knife in his hand. Dragging the blade across their throats would solve everything.

Otto tried to imagine it but he couldn't, couldn't force any coherent thought to form at all. Instead, he found himself thinking of his father standing next to him, gesturing to the Orloj and reminding him that each hour, every hour, the statues shook their heads in defiance of death. He wondered if it would hurt. He told himself that he hoped it would, but that was a lie.

What he really hoped was that it wouldn't be difficult. That he would be strong enough and fast enough and that no one would scream. That there wouldn't be much blood. What if the Man's throat was too thick? What if he woke up and slapped it away? Maybe, he supposed, he could just push the knife into the Man's chest instead... but if so, how should he grip it?

Otto felt his lower lip trembling. He sniffled and wiped at his nose before he caught himself. He'd never felt weaker, more helpless, more aware of his brief few years of life compared to the monstrous mechanism that was the world.

Maybe it would get easier after the first stab. Maybe he could just hold the knife above his head and bring it down into the sleeping face, again and again. Would it slit through the Man's eyes? Would it tear a hole in his cheeks, his skull, shear off chunks of his nose and punch gaps through his teeth?

Otto shifted his weight and the floor groaned. He flinched, bit his lip. His mouth was sticky and dry and that familiar taste of sour chalk turned his stomach. He knew every place to step up in the attic, what was safe and where, but down below was different, a strange middle land. He thought of the mouse droppings, the tiny streaking bodies darting nimbly back to safety. Vertigo returned in a stronger rush and he put a hand out to steady himself before remembering that he didn't dare touch a thing.

This was stupid. He was being stupid.

The absurd reality built inside him like a cresting wave.

He was in the room with them. *In the room with Them.*

Otto choked down a whimper, nearly gagged from terror as he backed away from the bed. A sudden urge to pee pressed a sharp, taut weight into his bladder and bruised flecks blossomed across his vision. The Man snorted in his sleep.

Otto ran.

Back down the hallway, through the library and past the book-shelf, ignoring the soft thumps of falling books as he slid the case back into place and bolted the door. He scurried up the staircase and flung himself onto the dingy mattress, collapsed into a quietly shaking heap. His face was wet with tears and his fists shook and he sucked at the air, felt it rasp in and out of his lungs in muffled, hitching sobs—sounds that filled the attic even as he tried to stop them, to choke them down and swallow them into silent death. Sounds that filled him with disgust.

He couldn't kill the Man. He couldn't even keep himself quiet. His parents would be so disappointed. He wiped at his tears and gripped the hilt of the knife, squeezed as hard as he could, until his knuckles drained to a bony white.

He needed to be smarter. To be better. To be stronger. There was no one else left but him.

He wished his hands were steady, were stone, that it wasn't blood in his veins but oil and grease. He wished that his muscles weren't frail and straining, but corded steel cables, gaskets, cogs. That the breath in his chest wouldn't race and stutter and catch with each shallow gulp of the empty night. He wished to be a killer, something dreadful, something unstoppable. Something inhuman.

He wished for a heart like a steel machine.

CHAPTER 10

OTTO woke long after midday, his mind fumbling through fog once more, his fingers wrapped around the hilt of the knife. He was hungry, painfully so. He chewed on one of the crackers that remained, but it was a tasteless, gritty offering that failed to satisfy him in any capacity, barely eased the pain in his stomach. He'd run out by the end of the week. With no one left to deliver more, his time was out. He sipped the last bit of water from the cup beside the mattress. He hadn't drawn up water the night before. The waste bucket was in need of emptying, but he wasn't sure when he'd next have the chance.

Never once did he set the knife down.

When he couldn't manage to lie still any longer, he crawled over to the stairs on his hands and knees. Splintered bits of wood dug into his palms as he descended, feet first, into the deeper gloom. At the bottom, he ran his fingers across the bare lumber back of the door. He'd repaired the lock and greased the door, but if anyone inspected the bookcase too closely, they'd see splinters from where crowbars had bitten into the wood. He closed his eyes and rested his forehead against the battered barrier that separated him from the world below. Distant voices reached him, but he couldn't make out the words.

The day before, he'd been terrified by their arrival. He'd hidden and waited and prayed they would pass him over, but they had not. His desire for them to leave hadn't left room for much else.

Today, he wanted to know more about them.

He slid the bolt and eased the door to the side. The day wasn't yet dark, but he didn't think the ghosts would show themselves now that he was no longer alone. *RUN*, his mother had said, but there was no running. There was nowhere to run to. Maybe there never had been. Instead, he crept closer to the hallway and listened to the sounds of life below.

He'd hidden from the faceless thing that haunted the daylight hours for weeks. How much harder could it be to hide from the living? He'd been practicing without ever realizing it.

Someone was cooking. The Woman, he supposed. He couldn't tell what she was cooking, but it was something on the stove top, something that smelled of garlic and salt and it breathed a yellow, living warmth into the air that he'd never noticed was absent. A soup, maybe. A hollow, starved pain simmered in his stomach. Homes were meant for more than hiding in dark attics. The Girl was downstairs too; their two voices climbed up from the kitchen, high and bright and oddly closer than he expected. Otto frowned at the thought until he remembered the hole in the bedroom floor that had once housed his father's speaker box.

He could listen without ever going downstairs. If they stayed in the dining room, he could even watch them. When he licked his lips, he thought he could taste the food in the air.

The porcelain clink of plates meeting metal cutlery rang out as he neared the Girl's room, the knife still clenched in his fist. The voices grew clearer.

A light in her room was on, and he flinched away from the artificial glow that bathed the room. A new lamp that Otto supposed they had brought with them. It emanated a subtle, dangerous buzzing that made Otto think of the stirring wings of hornets. The electricity was running again, must have been turned back on at some point. Otto wondered when it had. The water must be too. Not just whatever system fueled the toilet, but throughout the house. He could use the sink for his water, next time.

He made his way to the corner of her bedroom—*Mine! Not hers!*—and lowered himself to his hands and knees, leaned closer to the tiny eye of light and sound that peered down into the dining room below. Voices spilled up. They weren't as excited, now. It was easier to follow, reminded him far more of his mother's voice as she taught him German words alongside his Hebrew.

"Who did all this?" the Girl asked. She was wearing the same outfit as the night before, her hair a mess and her shoulders hunched as she hugged herself.

The two stood at either end of the broad wooden tabletop. Otto had scavenged the legs to support the golem's spine, but the top had been unmanageably heavy and he had been afraid of dropping it.

The Woman shrugged. She wore an unnaturally bright teal dress today, pleated lines running down from top to bottom. A slightly tattered red bandana wrapped her scalp. "Probably wanted the screws, or firewood. There's a shortage of everything these days. Get your end."

The two of them worked together to slide it up onto twin stacks of milk cartons. The cartons were new. Otto wondered if they'd eaten on the floor, the night before.

When the table was up on its new foundation, the Woman wiped at her brow and tucked a curled sprig of loose blonde hair up under her bandana, an intrinsically motherly gesture that said bizarre obstacles were to be anticipated and legless tables were just one of many she expected to encounter in a day.

"There's not a shortage of houses," the Girl muttered, but clearly enough that Otto could hear it with no difficulties. "Probably ones with furniture that isn't picked over."

"Birgitte," the Woman said. "Enough. Go bring in the dishes. Get them cleaned for dinner."

The Girl gave a long-suffering sigh and huffed on out. The front door swung open and then shut, and the Woman watched her go. When she was out of sight, the Woman's shoulders drooped and she pressed her palm to her forehead, an expression of weariness on her face. Otto felt something loosen inside himself.

When the Girl returned, the two of them retreated into the kitchen, out of sight. Otto pressed his face to the gap, his knees aching from the hard floor and his cheek sore. It was harder to understand them without seeing them. He didn't know why he cared what they had to say, but he couldn't drag himself away from the sound of human voices. Friendly voices, after so many weeks without.

He watched, and listened, and waited, and hated them. Hated their intrusion. Hated their crime. Hated how easily they fell into a routine. How easily they laughed.

By the time the Man came home, the sun had already drooped low behind the battlements of the high-roofed houses and the scent of baking bread had joined the warm smell from the kitchen. Otto barely had time to crawl to the banister vantage point to watch him step out from the front closet, still dressed in his coat and tie, a newspaper tucked under one arm. The others called out a welcome to him and he headed toward the kitchen without bothering to wash the sooty black from his face.

"Renée. Birge," he said.

Renée. Birgitte. The Woman. The Girl. When the Woman emerged and placed the bowls of food at the table, her bandana was gone, her hair carefully arranged in blonde ringlets and a smile locked onto her face. Not soup after all, some sort of dumplings in a loose orange broth. Fresh bread balanced against the edge of the bowls, the crust cracked and flaking and chestnut brown. Otto bit his tongue to keep a hungry, wet sound inside himself but the sensation ate away at him in turn, burrowed deeper into his gut with furious scrabbling claws. Not just food, but *real* food. Food made with warmth, flavor, meat. Juices. Blood. Food that provided so much more than the dry, pitiful crackers.

Otto's knees let out an aching protest almost as sharp as the pain in his stomach as he hunched over the hole in the floor. As he watched them sit and carelessly stuff their faces while he starved. The Man shoveled his dinner down before propping up the newspaper in front of himself, studying it instead of his family beyond.

"How long do you think we're going to be here?" the Girl asked, when her bowl was half empty. She poked listlessly at what remained. Otto's stomach clenched, hot with the red bite of acid and nothing to fill it. "I wish…" she trailed off.

The Man folded his newspaper over and peered toward his daughter.

"I swear, Birge. If you're still moping about the damn cat…"

"We just left him there."

"We couldn't afford to feed it even if we wanted to."

"You said the rations didn't matter to us. That's why you run the factories, so that—"

"I work where I'm told to, when I'm told to, to feed *you*. Not to feed stray cats."

"Frank," the Woman said. She gave him a meaningful glance.

He shrugged, then dipped his head in lukewarm surrender. "Damn thing was half wild anyway. All cats are. If it wanted to come with us, it'd be here. Can't blame it. This city wasn't my choice either."

He flicked the newspaper as he brought it back up. The flutter of the paper reminded Otto so clearly of the sound of the kite snapping in the wind that he found himself clenching his teeth. A cat. A stray cat. Otto's head began to throb. They invaded his home, sat eating their dinner just below where his parents were murdered, and talked about some *pet* they used to have.

"There are people who have it far worse than we do, Birgitte," the Woman said. "I'm sure he'll be fine."

"If things keep going the way they've been going, that cat'll be luckier than us all," the Man muttered. "Until someone eats the damn thing."

Birgitte let out an outraged squawk.

"Frank!" The Woman said. "Things will turn around," she told the Girl. "The rationing will let up. The radio said we're doing better. The Russians—"

The Man grunted and she fell off.

"Can I go to my room?" Birgitte asked.

"Clean up first," the Woman said.

The Girl picked up her bowl, gave a furious glare that her father ignored, then marched her bowl off toward the kitchen, the ceramic not yet licked clean. Food, about to be turned into waste. Otto's face throbbed from where it pressed against the floor.

Time was up. Otto pushed himself to his feet, away from the smell, the sound, the flutter of life, and just like that he made his decision.

Tonight, he would kill them.

Not on impulse. Not because he was scared, but because he was furious. One by one, and none would be spared. The Man, the Woman, the Girl. Forget the metal construction above, he'd be his father's golem. He would paint his face in blood and his hand wouldn't hesitate. His fist wouldn't shake. He'd stab and hurt and kill them, put the knife in their faces and necks until they were as dead as his mother and father, until their beds were wet with the death, until there was nothing left but his rage, and he'd scream it out in a red tide of ruin. Then, after that, he'd eat whatever food was left. There was no need to plan beyond that. That would be enough.

His hands were ancient again, he realized. The scars stood out white in the twilight glow, the thin silvery hairs like coils of barbed wire across the liver-spotted flesh beneath.

He didn't let himself flinch away from the sight, from the thought. As he slipped back up the stairs into the attic, he dared the ghosts to challenge him. The faceless woman, the dark man, the monsters below, any of them. Time itself. Let all of them do their worst. He was haunted already. Now it was his turn to do the haunting.

And after tonight there'd be more spirits to add to the number.

CHAPTER 11

HE waited by the window, listening to the Orloj toll out their final hours.

When the night had taken full swing and he heard no more sounds from below, he readied himself. He sat, cross-legged, in front of the golem, his father's journal in front of him, his nightshirt in a bundle in his lap. The air was chilly and set a whisper of bumps across the skin stretched taut over jutting bone, but he didn't want to risk nicking his shirt when he had so few left. Carefully, very carefully, he dragged the stolen blade along the back of his arm in one short jerk. A tiny whimper escaped before he could bite it back. The cut was thin, shallow, hot, and the red took some time to trickle down until he could smear enough on his fingers. Without a mirror, he had to watch himself in the construct's polished metal knees as he traced the symbols onto his forehead by candlelight.

Emét.

The word that meant truth. The word that was one letter away from death. No fear. What did he need the golem for? He could do everything himself.

The thing towered above him, headless, the shadows of the rafters heavy around its shoulders, as if the darkness itself were its face, and the face was indeed watching the boy who sat in front of it. He pressed his nightshirt against the cut on his wrist until the pain stopped, until the bleeding slowed—how little blood he seemed to have—and then he tugged it back over his head. Streaks of red crisscrossed the dull blue that had turned mostly gray from grime and oil stains. He imagined the family in the rooms below him picking out their own nightclothes, the last they'd ever wear.

No, he didn't need the golem at all. He would be his father's creation. He would be the one to erase the intruders. He wouldn't sit, unmoving, while they celebrated their victory.

The helplessness from the night before was gone. The knife with its hateful symbol was an anchor that kept him grounded and he hefted it, tossed it lightly, snatched it out of the air as he waited. He thought of the kite jerking out of his grip beneath the bright sky, but this time it wasn't a longing, it was just a memory of another thing they'd stolen from him. He had a new foundation, now. A new purpose. He felt ready. He felt *right*.

He snuffed out the candle.

He eased the bookshelf open as gently as he could.

The door made no more noise than its shadow as he let it close behind him. He gave the room a cursory check for the ghosts, but there was no one there to answer his challenge. The whole house was silent, sleeping, defenseless. Everything was right where he needed it to be, where it was *supposed* to be—

Almost everything.

One thing was not.

On the piano's chair, a pair of dumplings were waiting for him on a napkin, next to a ragged slice of bread.

CHAPTER 12

OTTO never made it farther than the library, that night.

He waited, the knife in his fist, crouched beside the bookshelf for what seemed like forever before he finally risked a step closer.

The dumplings were cold, of course, but the idea of eating a homecooked meal, of real meat instead of the flat crackers, filled his stomach with a sharp, awful heat that outweighed even his plans for murder. A story from the synagogue about men crying out to God for more than manna came to mind, but he couldn't organize the thought into sense. He should leave the food where it was. It could be poisoned, or a trap, or simply a bizarre carelessness by the new intruders that they might remember when sunrise came around.

It could be any number of things, but he knew in his heart it wasn't. The food was left out for him. Knish, just like she used to make for him after a long day, her lavender perfume and the sight of her smile so vibrant and clear that everything else around him seemed to fade to hazy imagining by comparison.

Ilsa?

The memory fell apart. It was hard, at night, to think. As if the gloom of the sleeping house was leeching into his mind. Maybe that's why the ghosts kept to the mornings, he supposed. It didn't matter anyway. The food was there and it was real and when he couldn't resist any longer, he crept forward, scooped up the napkin and retreated back into the attic stairwell.

He locked the bookshelf door behind himself, sat in the darkness, and gorged himself. The skin of the dumplings was wet, greasy, loose. The insides—more potato than meat as he'd imagined it—were soggy and saturated into mush. He gulped it down without the slightest hesitation. Juices ran down his chin and he licked at himself, scooped any stray spatters with dirty fingers and sucked them clean. The bread, next. Every bite of it was delicious.

He didn't make it up to his mattress. He wasn't sure if eating their food was a betrayal or not, but the thought of the headless golem looming over him while he stuffed his face made him suddenly uncomfortable. More than uncomfortable. His lower lip trembled and he bit down on it to keep the tears stifled down.

"I'm sorry," he whispered into the black weight of the attic above. He fumbled around for the candle and the matches he had stashed there, counted their dwindling number with his fingertips. So few matches left, but he lit one anyway, set it against the wick. If it really was a trap, he wouldn't need the spares.

But no feet came thundering toward his secret doorway, no exultant cries shouted out as guns were readied and checked. Just silence, aside from his chewing and the gentle creak of the sleeping house. The smell of boiled meat and the taste of salt on his tongue, like sweat.

If it wasn't a trap, then could it be a mistake? That seemed unlikely. Someone had slipped into the library and left the food. That wasn't accidental. It was intentional. It was for him. Someone knew the secret that was his life, and that thought banished all plans of violence. He was seen and known. But by who?

Ilsa?

That name again, but no further clues beyond an odd feeling of sadness. Not the furious grief of losing his parents, but a deep wistfulness.

He licked crumbs from his hands and from the napkin, then sat running his hand over the flat of the knife's blade and staring at the back of the bookshelf doorway. His arm ached. In the distance, thunder gently rumbled, although it might have been warplanes for all Otto knew.

He waited, lost in thought, until he realized he was dozing off and the night had slipped half by. He wiped the blood from his forehead and pressed his shirt against his arm until the pain dulled and the cloth gummed to his flesh. He climbed the stairs. When he cuddled up against the metal fist to sleep, he told himself it wasn't clenched even tighter in fury at his weakness.

But in his dreams, he was again in the kitchen, the oven open and the ruined mice inside. Only, this time he scooped them out with his bare hands. This time he packed them into his mouth, one hairy little body after the next, until he gagged, until their wriggling, scrabbling limbs clawed at the back of his throat and their squeaks muffled into ticks and clicks as their tiny bones popped apart.

And when he bit down they burst like over-ripe fruit, and he delighted in the delicious bloody rush until he woke up, weeping.

CHAPTER 13

EACH night, a new offering of food awaited him.

A small offering taken from their dinners, a slim fragment of their laughter and warmth and conversation pared off in secret and left out for him. He couldn't be sure which of them left it, or why, and with no way to look out into the library he had no way to safely check.

No longer did he crouch above them each evening as they ate, peering through the tiny gap and feeling himself knotting up with envy and hatred. Now he waited with anticipation. The boiled potatoes and vegetables they ate for dinner showed up later that night with a small serving of bread and marmalade. When he saw the schnitzel served the following night, he rubbed his hands together in wild, lunatic glee. The food wasn't prepared the way his mother had insisted, was probably forbidden, but he found it hard to care. If God was that concerned, he shouldn't have taken her from him.

When he wasn't eating, he was thinking about it. He spent hours each day imagining the next meal, savoring the memory of the night before. The scraps weren't enough to satisfy him, but after so long with so little, they were almost enough. When he dreamed, he dreamt of mice.

The first night, he'd waited and watched the napkin for hours before taking it. The second night, he barely hesitated. By the fourth night, those glorious dumplings again, he was salivating with jittery desire in the dark stairwell as the sounds of stillness and sleep made their claim over the house.

The simple act of hope, of wanting, blazed inside him.

His belly filled, he set to work again.

The golem seemed to revitalize too, despite his nightly betrayal. He had to work carefully and quietly, but he was used to that. Light was a bigger problem. The nights had grown cloudy now that spring was in full swing, and Otto had only one candle left. The only matches that remained were the ones he'd found in the kitchen cache so long before, a half dozen splintered sticks with sulfurous heads that hissed when struck. Otto had to risk working during the daylight hours.

During the night, after eating, he crept only as far as the bathroom to refill his cups of water. He didn't dare risk exploring further, didn't allow himself to slip down and check if there was any more food tucked away. Whoever left out the offerings was aware of his existence, but the others were not or there would be no need for secrecy. He couldn't risk it, not yet, and too often he heard the Man stir in the night, wander down to the lower floor to poke around the kitchen. The waste bucket was half full and the smell had become something loud and foul, but he didn't yet dare dump it into the toilet. The flush might attract too much attention. Soon, he told himself. Soon.

He had already repaired the base of the golem, but now he fitted the stepladder onto its chest as a breastplate, the wooden rungs like exposed ribs that he had to climb to reassemble the shoulders. The lamp lay beneath the rungs, a heart in its ancient cage. The arms themselves were undamaged, as he'd expected, but he had to remove each piece, carry it up and set it carefully into place, fitting the teeth of the cogs into each other, the plated steel in proper layers and snapped into place. He attached the base of the head, but the face still lay in a dented ruin on the floor.

On the fifth night, he didn't bother taking the knife with him as he listened to the Orloj toll midnight and he made his way down.

He slid the door open and stepped out, and before the bookcase had settled shut behind him, he realized his mistake.

A figure waited for him, watched him from the far corner beside the hallway door. The man in black, he thought at first, grinning with a mouth full of sparks, his belly an incinerator, a crematorium, the cigarette in his fingers trailing a thread of iron-gray smoke. Then it was the faceless ghost, Ilsa, her eyes flat and staring, her mouth opened into a black cavern, into a silent, hideous scream. Ms. Fena. All of them, gathered into one single form, all of them waiting, watching. Their trap, sprung.

"*Found you,*" the voice said. "*Don't run.*" It might have been a multitude of voices or one, but Otto couldn't say because the ghosts vanished just as quickly as he'd seen them. In their place, in that far corner, she stood watching.

The Girl.

CHAPTER 14

"**D**ON'T run," she said again. "I'm Birgitte. What's your name?"

She stood in the corner by the door, chewing on her lip, nearly invisible among the gloom. A pale, ruffled nightgown hung from her shoulders. Ethereal strands of runaway hair formed a loosely twisted crown. Her feet were bare. In the dim illumination of moonlight, she might as well have been a ghost herself.

Otto stared at the Girl. His legs felt as if they were carved from stone or forged from plated metal, someone else's body that could not move or act on its own.

"I'm not going to hurt you. I promise," she said. She spoke slowly, enunciating each word. "Do you speak German? My Czech is not very good."

You be careful of her. That one will hurt you.

His father's voice, but a faint echo and quickly extinguished. His heartbeat hammered through his chest, an unrelenting piston that tore into him and choked his breath, drowned his thoughts, left him feeling dizzy and stuporous. Shadows pressed in from the edges of his vision, creeping toward him as he slipped further into their grip.

"I speak German. Please…" Otto said. They were the first words he'd spoken to another human being in weeks, and they came out wobbly and squeaking. His thoughts flickered to the sound from the stove, those tiny shrieks of terror and death as the flame roared up beneath them.

Birgitte clapped her hands together in delight. "Wonderful! What is your name?"

All that was left was for her to call out and the Man would come bulling in and drag him kicking and screaming to the train station where he'd turn into smoke. He clenched his hands into fists, wished for the weight of the knife in them, but it was upstairs, tucked beneath his mattress. How had he been so careless? So stupid? Of course they knew he was taking the food, that's why they left it there. It was a trap, had always been a trap, a steel-toothed monster that bit down hard enough to crack bone and slice through tendon. He willed himself to charge toward her before she could raise her voice, but his feet refused to obey. Hopelessness settled on him like a comforting blanket. Acceptance was easier. Death was easier. All he really wanted to do was sit down.

"Otto," he said, barely more than a whisper. "My name is Otto. Please don't kill me."

Even if he had the knife, it wouldn't matter. Like the ghosts, all his plans for violence had been banished, had limped off to dark recesses in the presence of an actual person who was more than just a sleeping lump. His lower lip trembled and he bit against it to steady himself.

"Kill? I would never. Please don't cry, Otto. I hope you liked the food? I didn't know what you liked." She spoke with an upwards lilt, her hands pressed together as if in prayer, and Otto realized she was scared too. Not like him, but still nervous, and the common ground filled him with a sudden desire to comfort her.

"I liked it."

She gave a sigh of relief. "I'm glad you did. Father says we have to tell people we're following the rations, but his position helps him get extra food. He's the *obermeister* at a factory. I don't know that word in Czech. Do you know it in German? It means he is in charge. It's just you, right? Living up there? Don't worry. I won't tell anyone you're here."

He struggled to follow the tumble of her words.

"How...?"

"I heard you that first day. It was either that or ghosts and I don't believe in ghosts. Do you?" She didn't wait for Otto's answer. "If there were ghosts, I think they'd be awfully bored. And I'm definitely sure ghosts don't eat food you leave out for them. So I figured it was someone. I'm glad you're a kid."

She took a step forward and he flinched, but instead of laying a hand on him she sat on the piano bench, her back to the keys, and patted the spot beside her. He obeyed. A moment later she fished a balled-up wet napkin out of her pocket and placed its surprising weight into his hands.

For a moment he thought he saw the scar carving a path across his palm, but then it was gone and he was just himself, a boy holding a boiled potato wrapped in limp cabbage and doing his best to not cram the entire thing in his mouth in one ambitious bite. He hadn't liked cabbage, before the war. That shouldn't have mattered, but it was food he had just traded his life for. There wasn't even much of it.

Then again, his wasn't much of a life.

"What are you going to do to me?" he asked.

Birgitte cocked her head. "I'm not going to *do* anything to you Otto. I just wanted to say hello. We're neighbors, right? So, hello." She reached out and touched his shoulder with one fingertip as if to see if he was real. He stared at her and all at once he was conscious of her age, of how pretty she was, of how dirty and small he felt beside her.

"Hello," he said.

She grinned. "You can eat, you know. Don't worry about my parents. They sleep like they're dead."

Tears came, silent and warm against his cheeks as he took a timid bite. The cabbage tasted orange, oniony and oversalted. He smeared his face dry with the back of his hand.

Birgitte touched his shoulder again, gentler this time, a placating gesture to calm a skittish wild animal.

"I know you're scared but it's going to be alright." She smiled, took one of the chunks of potato from his lap and popped it in her mouth. Otto fought back the urge to yank the napkin away from her, and a second, even more confusing desire to offer her the whole meal. "I've heard the rumors too. You know, about what they do out there." She gestured vaguely toward the front of the house. "I don't know how much of it is true or not but I know my *Vati* wouldn't hurt you. He's not like that. He's a good man. He just works at a factory."

Otto thought of the knife he had tucked away, the hideous symbol on its hilt.

That one will hurt you.

"Please don't tell him about me," he said.

"I won't. I won't tell anyone at all. I'd rather drop dead. I'll keep you safe, okay?"

Otto nodded. He took a bite and chewed and swallowed. He wished for water to wash it down, but he didn't tell her. He wasn't sure why he didn't. Birgitte continued on.

"Just don't ask me to come up with a story for why you're here, okay? I'm not good at lying. Is the food good? I helped mom cook."

Otto nodded again. He knew she had. He'd listened to her rummage around in the kitchen and hated her for her happiness. "Thank you," he said.

She brightened up. "I'll bring you more tomorrow. Do you need anything else up there?" She gestured at the bookcase door, still cracked. He wondered what he'd do if she tried to go up. He knew what his parents would want him to do, but they were gone. The dead asked for so much but offered so little.

"No," he said. "I'm okay."

"Well, then, I'm going to bed. It's late. Next time don't wait so late to come on down, so I'm not as tired. I hope we can talk again soon. Friends?"

"Friends," Otto said quietly. She reached for the napkin and he reluctantly surrendered it. He'd hoped to check it for crumbs.

"Goodnight, Otto."

Then she was gone. A moment later, he heard the quiet click of her door closing. Otto sat among the heavy shadows and told himself that, no matter what, next time he was bringing the knife.

CHAPTER 15

BUT he didn't.

"You may just be the first friend I've made in the last year," Birgitte confided in him, several days later. "No, really. We lived in Essen before the war, and then in Schweinfurt, but I never really liked the people in Schweinfurt. Mom wouldn't send me to the schools there, either. She taught me at home. I miss school."

Otto nodded along to the sound of her voice as he chewed. Following her words was getting easier, little by little, but it still took him a few moments to understand and by then he was trying to catch up with whatever new topic she had reached. Speaking was far more difficult, but she rarely paused long enough for it to matter, and he had no particular need to try. She was a fountain of life, pouring herself into him, and he simply drank.

"What I really miss is roulade. Do you know roulade? It's this thin pork rolled around vegetables and fried, and with gravy… well, it's the best dinner you'll ever have. You've got to try it, you know. Proper strudel, too, although Mom says there's no cream available," she informed him, nodding in solemn agreement with herself. "Strudel isn't the same without cream. I can't see why cows have such strong opinions about war that we can't get cream."

Birgitte seemed built from contradictions. She was pretty, but unkempt. During the day she was quiet and studious and patient in her lessons, but in the quiet afterdark she was a constant source of chatter, babbling about one topic or another, seemingly at random—the rationing, the war, her friends, her favorite music, the movies she'd seen and the books she read. He wondered if she thought of him much at all, during the daylit hours, but he supposed it didn't matter so long as she remembered to bring him dinner. She ate quite a bit of it while they talked, too.

"Of course it won't matter. That's what *Vati* says. He says the newspapers are all wrong. Cows or no cows, the war is going badly. Really badly. That's why we had to move, because Essen got bombed, and Schweinfurt wasn't safe anymore. They got bombed too. Prague is safe, at least."

For who? Otto wondered, but he didn't say anything. He didn't want to know what side she thought was her own. Instead, he watched the lines of her lips, of her collarbone and the way the corners of her mouth dipped slightly downward when she smiled. The blue of her eyes.

The rest of the world was a cage. The mornings continued to blur past in hazy dreams, and the nights afterward seemed to dull in the afterglow, but for that stretch of dark when the house was quiet aside from her and he ate his dinner, he was the closest he had been to happiness in a long, long time. He watched, and he listened, and for a few minutes the world's grim monotony shattered.

The Man and the Woman had a very simple routine, too. He left early, sometimes stirring before Otto went to sleep, and arrived back home as the Orloj chimed five. He ate, read, and continued reading as Otto retreated to the attic. He spoke only a little, seemed caught up in his own world and went to bed with the sunset. The Woman spent hours each day cooking, cleaning, working the house back into something serviceable, and when she wasn't, she invariably spent long stretches teaching Birgitte. Sometimes they held their afternoon lessons in the library, and Otto crept down the attic stairs to listen, perched on the steps, as she instructed Birgitte about mathematics and coached her through reading the Czech books left on the bookcase, but most days those lessons stopped early with the Woman muttering about the room's smell.

"They don't like to come in here. They keep the door closed during the day, open at night to air it out," Birgitte informed him. "If anyone ever hears us, I'll tell them I'm in here reading at night, out loud to myself," Birgitte said. "If you ever need to… you know, use the bathroom or wash up, you can let me know."

She gave him a meaningful glance, but not one that Otto could translate. He nodded mutely. He tried to imagine her standing guard while he carried the bucket of shit down to the toilet and it made him feel vaguely ill.

Most of his days were simply spent waiting, counting the minutes as they spilled into hours, and ignoring the jagged hunger that boiled in his belly. The golem hunched, unfinished and unimpressed with his fascination. His father's journal lay untouched, the pages still arranged around it, although Otto couldn't remember why he had arranged them any particular way. He hadn't worked on the golem since he had spoken with Birgitte. The creation was so close to complete—a few more pieces screwed into place and figuring out how to repair and attach the face—but now it all seemed frivolous and artificial. His mother was right. It was just a pile of junk. An abomination. A hulking, ugly lump of faceless night.

Birgitte might as well have been the rising of the sun.

One time, she touched his hand while they sat, side by side, on the piano bench. Most nights, she gave him a ginger, body-separated hug before going back to her room. Even if she wrinkled her nose while she did it, the feel of her arms around him, her warm body so near to him, somehow both soft and bony at the same time, filled him with a crazed, desperate flare of joy that lit up the rest of his night.

Some days, when he couldn't sleep or sit silently anymore and the constant hunger boiled in his gut, he pretended she was there and talking to him. That she was telling him that his parents had been taken to the hospital and were okay. Sometimes she told him she loved him. Sometimes she just sang his mother's lullaby and held him until he realized it was his own voice, low and squeaky from disuse.

Otto realized his entire world had become adjusted to their presence, to the rhythm of their day. The sound of her voice became as familiar as the Orloj. His nightly dinners weren't enough to stave off hunger through the day, but they made it tolerable. Her hushed laughter filled in just enough to keep himself from running empty. And the distant thunder grew more frequent.

Then, the Man no longer came home at five, but at six. New voices plagued the daytime, German speakers who never stayed too long and who Otto never got to see. Planes cut the sky, and distant rumbles resonated in the pit of his stomach as often as not. The horizon smudge of smoke seemed darker, even as spring bloomed in full.

Otto no longer dared sneak out at night. Birgitte filled his water cup from the sink. The bucket climbed dangerously close to full. For all Otto wished he could steal more food to eat, there was simply too much risk. The Man woke earlier and earlier, paced the house for hours before sunrise, mumbling and irritable. Cars traveled down the streets at strange times. The streetlights were extinguished.

Soon, it took the Man until seven to arrive home, and Otto could no longer spend his evenings watching the Woman prepare dinner. The meals were smaller, and she waited, half at the ready or strolling through the house for hours, waiting for his return. Birgitte spent more time in her room, too, and Otto crept down only after they had already begun eating to avoid them both and keep his dinnertime vigil.

One night, he had dozed off when the eighth chime pushed him awake and he heard the Man in the front hallway. Otto rubbed the sleep from his eyes, spat the gnawing hunger from his mouth and crept on down. The weight of the knife tucked into his tool belt helped him pull himself to attention.

Voices from below drifted up through the hole beside Birgitte's bed. The Woman asking the Man about his day. The low grumble of his voice, half lost beneath the clatter of silverware. Dinner was well underway and Otto breathed in the smell—warm and salty and delicious—as he made his way down the hallway. He tossed the knife into the air, caught it by the wooden handle and tossed it gently upward again as he contemplated the scent from below. It smelled like schnitzel, but he hoped it was dumplings. They didn't hold together all that well and when they got cold they turned greasy, but he didn't care. They were the first bite of fresh meat he'd had after living so long on bread and canned soup and crackers, and he couldn't imagine he'd ever get tired of the taste.

He lofted the knife up again as he stepped into the bedroom and then froze in place.

He had never seen the room before.

CHAPTER 16

OTTO stared, his mind unable to process what he was seeing. Nothing looked right. Nothing was where it had been the day before. The stenciled animals that lined the ceiling were gone. The sentry line of broken clocks had been removed. There was still a bed, but it was different. Different sheets, different covers, different frame. Not just different. *Wrong.*

An ugly, low moan stretched its way up from inside his chest and he pressed his hands to the sides of his head, but his hands were different too. His hair felt oddly similar to silk, to spiderweb, something nearly insubstantial. His fingernails, cracked and scabby, dug into the skin of his scalp that was suddenly as dry and thin as paper. When he looked down, he saw he was wearing some sort of long tan pants, brown leather shoes long faded from use.

A divot had been hacked into the floor next to his foot.

The knife. Where is the knife?

If he knew where the knife was, the rest of it would make sense, some part of his mind insisted. He needed an anchor, something solid that made sense. He had thrown it upwards and... when he looked up, it was still falling, falling, end over end. Time slowed with each revolution. It seemed, for a moment, that he could trace his eyes across the terrible black windmill, the glint of the polished blade, the ugly, wicked point, each detail of the weapon pronounced in perfect clarity as it plummeted toward the ground, past his legs—once more he was barefoot and dressed in his drawstring pajamas—and slammed into the floor beside him with an awful twanging thud.

Directly into the slot where the divot had been just a moment ago.

And just that quickly, the room was back to normal. The animals, the clocks, all of them had returned. The lazy dinnertime chatter below had not.

"What was that?" he heard the Man say. His chair scraped back as he stood.

They're coming. The thought pounded an iron spike through Otto's confusion and he had half turned to run before he remembered the knife. He dropped to one knee and tugged on it, but it stayed seated in the wood. *They're coming They're coming They're coming.* His mind tumbled through the loop, and it was no longer dumplings he smelled but the reek of his own urine, the sharp bite of gun smoke as he cowered inside the golem's belly.

He gripped the knife with both hands, placed his feet and heaved upwards. The blade sprang up out of the floorboard, left a massive slot gouged into the wood, but he didn't have time to think about it because the Man was no longer in the dining room, had entered the front hall and Otto didn't dare step back toward the library.

There was no way to step back into the hallway without being seen. No way to slip back into the library. *The door to the attic. Did I leave it open?*

"No. No. No," he whispered. His prayer did nothing to dispel the horror of the Man climbing the stairs. He looked around the bedroom but there were so few places to hide, so little furniture. He had to be fast, but being quiet was as important. He forced his lips to press together, held back the scream swelling inside him.

The bed.

As quietly as he could, he dropped onto his belly and wormed his way down among the dust and boxes and pairs of scuffed shoes. He barely fit, could scarcely draw half a breath before the weight of the bed above him pressed back. He gripped the knife close to his heart and tried his best to still his shivering as the Man stepped into the room.

Birgitte followed a moment later, fluttering along after him. Otto watched their legs move closer, her slippered feet, his work-boots with their metal tips.

"What are you worried about? I'm sure it's nothing, *Vati*," she said. "Just a… something fell over."

"Nothing is over." He paused. "And what's that smell?"

"I don't know. Maybe it's nothing?"

The Man grunted. "Nothing doesn't smell. Maybe it's a mouse. They said the house was empty for weeks, I guess there's bound to be something."

"*Echt?*" Birgitte said. "A mouse is living in my room? That's really gross."

He grunted again. "Not living, no. Not by the smell, at least."

The Man's boots stepped closer and it was too easy for Otto to imagine it was the other man, the man in black, the man who carried fire inside him and left thunderous ruin along with his laughter, that bloody-mouthed, snarling demon come to torment him. To offer him hope and scraps of dinner only to snatch them away.

What had happened to the room?

Something was wrong. Awfully, dreadfully wrong. For one blurry moment Otto could almost see the strange room again. That it wasn't the Man. That it wasn't the dark man either. That it was *her*.

Ilsa.

The two images were weaved together, overlapped like the old photographs when the subjects moved too quickly. The Man was still talking to Birgitte, but Ilsa was kneeling down beside the bed, tilting her head to peer under at him.

"*There you are, Otto,*" she said. Only her voice wasn't mocking. It wasn't even unkind. Her face was no bloody ruin. It was plain, wrinkled with age, unremarkable but oddly appealing. Her nose was a little crooked. Her chin marked with a thin scar. Her eyes were bright, light blue, almost the same silver gray as her hair. *"Found you."*

He did not dare make a sound, just watched her, trembling and terrified as she squeezed in next to him and touched his hand with her own. He clenched his eyes shut, ignored the smell of lavender and waited for whatever horror would come slouching toward him next.

"Otto?"

He opened his eyes.

Birgitte's voice. The room was darker. She spoke softly, but it was undeniably her. Ilsa had vanished completely. The house felt firmly familiar again. He wiped at his mouth to drive off the taste.

"Otto?" she asked again. "Are you still in here?"

He whimpered a sound in answer as he scuttled out from under the bed.

Birgitte stood over him, frowning down. "Otto. You can't do that. You can't be in here. This is my room," she said. "He could've caught you. Do you know how mad he'd be at me? You have to stay in your room until they're asleep. You can't ever do that again. Do you understand?"

Otto felt his head bob up and down in agreement. If he spoke, he'd start crying and he didn't want to cry, needed to not cry, not in front of her. If he started, he might never stop. He swallowed down against the awful mixture of relief and terror that rose in a poisonous bubble from his belly. *That one will hurt you.* The thought, in his father's voice, filtered in, unwelcome. *She's mad at you. It's her room now. She's going to tell them about you. She's going to turn you in and they'll come and drag you down the stairs, they'll put knives in you or shoot you or beat you until you're broken and turn you into smoke in the train to Chelmno—*

Birgitte seemed to take his silence as contrition and sighed, gave her head a pretty shake. "Oh Otto. I couldn't think of a way to distract him. I'm no good at lying. He's not mean, I promise. He was just scared. Let's get you back to your room and no more... whatever it is you were doing in here. Okay?"

Otto nodded again, but she already had her head poked out the door into the hallway to see if it was clear.

Never again. Watching them eat and hearing about the world beyond the cramped little attic had been one of his only joys for weeks now, but it seemed such a reasonable thing to give up. He wondered if there ever came a point when you stopped having to give things up.

Ilsa. It was her fault. She had done something very strange in the room, had caused him to drop the knife. And he had, hadn't he? He had thrown it up... he looked down at the gouge in the floorboards. He had seen the notch *before* the knife had landed. His head ached. The fade of adrenaline left him dizzy, too weak to even attempt to assemble the pieces of the puzzle.

"Come on, Otto," Birgitte whispered to him, beckoned him with a click of her tongue and a tilt of her head. "Let's get you back home."

CHAPTER 17

"**H**ERE you are," she said as she opened the door.

Otto darted inside. For a moment, he'd been afraid the library would have transformed too, but no, the room was the same as it always had been, the same as he'd left it. The doorway to the attic was still cracked, the sliver of dark leaking out its dull, ugly smell. If the Man or the Woman had checked... but they hadn't. He'd gotten lucky.

Birgitte took her usual seat at the piano bench and Otto sank down beside her. She set a fried sliver of some unidentified meat in his hand, golden brown and mouthwateringly crisp.

"Sorry, it's the only thing I had grabbed when you... what is it that you did, anyway? Why do you have my dad's knife? He's been looking for it you know. A friend gave it to him for all the work he did at the factories."

"I was thirsty. I just... I went the wrong way," he said. It sounded insultingly stupid, but he didn't know what else to say. He thought she was going to ask him for the knife, but instead she looked past him toward the cracked door.

"What's it like up there? You've been in my room. Can I come up and see?"

Otto flinched. The idea of her, with her pretty smile and pretty bows and clean clothes coming up to the mausoleum of the attic brought on an ugly, nauseating pang of shame. Some things simply couldn't be shared.

If she goes upstairs, she'll die. The thought flashed into his mind with sudden, awful certainty, and left just as quickly.

"That's okay," she said quickly. "I shouldn't have asked."

"No, it's okay. But it's not a place for you," Otto said. *And it smells like shit,* he nearly added.

She sighed. She broke one of the crispy edges from the schnitzel in his hands and popped it in her mouth, then continued with her mouth still full. "Everyone feels that way about Germans, here. They say, 'It's not a place for you,' and tell us to leave. Mom says I can't go outside alone, not for so much as a stroll in the park. Prague is a cruel city. It's pretty, but the people here don't much like us, do they?"

Otto remembered his Ms. Fena and the red and white and black windmill flag she'd waved as the parade rolled past his bedroom window. That ugly, sneering grin she'd had plastered on her withered old face as she saw him looking down.

That one will hurt you.

"I like you," he said. It felt like he was confessing a crime and he wished he hadn't said it, but he wasn't quite sure why. His father would be so ashamed.

She blushed. "Well, Otto, I bring you food. You have to like me."

Otto tried to think of a response, but she didn't wait for it. She chattered on, rolled past him before he could fumble at the words in German, not that he would've had much hope if she gave him forever to try. He didn't even know the words in Czech. But he noticed her flush didn't quite go away, and when she left, it was later than usual.

And then there was nothing left to do but to return upstairs, to where the golem waited, a black shape towering among the rancid gloom.

"Is that all we're worth to you?"

His father's voice. Otto startled, searching for the source. He hoped to find some apparition, just to see his father's face again, but the words came from the floor. From the stain, he thought at first... but no. From the speaker box lying beside the golem's severed face.

"Papa?"

The speaker crackled with dull static, an old radio reaching out across a fathomless distance. *"Otto. Is that all we're worth to you? A few table scraps?"*

"It's not like that," Otto mumbled.

"Then why are you whispering?"

He sniffled. "She's not bad. She likes me. You don't know her."

"That one will hurt you. She's going to kill you," his mother's whisper rasped out beside his father's. *"She's going to kill you. She's going to kill you..."*

"She's nice to me. She brought me food."

"She murdered us. She'll murder you. She's one of the monsters. The world is full of them. And you hold her hand," his father snarled. *"I made you for a reason. And when it came down to my moment of need..."*

"Stop it!" Otto pleaded, his voice cracking from the strain. He clapped a hand over his mouth. He'd spoken. Not a whisper, but an actual full-bodied word. He waited in stunned silence, shocked at his carelessness. No sound answered him from below. Only his mother's reply. No longer angry, but tired and growing further and further away.

"They'll never stop coming for you, little lamb..."

"It's going to end soon. You don't know anything." He looked around the attic for some evidence to support him. Some scrap that could bolster his claim. All he saw was garbage and ruin. Clothing tangled in heaps where it had sat for weeks. Tools and scraps, still piled beside the metal man. The filthy bucket full of dark fluid and the lump-spattered floor around it. The stained mattress gone threadbare. The sacks hanging listlessly from their hooks, contents dumped on the floor as he searched for food. "It has to end, doesn't it?"

"Poor Otto. This thing is never going to end," the voices whispered, together. *"Never."*

CHAPTER 18

"**H**ITLER'S dead," Birgitte said.

Otto stared at her, the packet of food in his hands momentarily forgotten. It weighed far less than the offerings used to. She'd folded the ends under and wrapped it like a present, complete with a little bow. Ever since the night when he said he liked her, she'd taken to wrapping them. "He's not dead. He'll never be dead."

She shook her head, curls bobbing in the candlelight. She'd brought and lit one from the house below, assured him that no one would notice the light. It made him nervous all the same. "He is. It's all over the radio. *Vati* says that it means the war is over. The fighting will stop and no more..." she waved a slim-wristed hand as if the atrocities of the last three years were lined up in gallery behind her, waiting to be dismissed.

Otto expected some rush of relief, exhilaration, anything at all. He tugged at the bow, unfolded the napkin, looked at the wedge of dark, half-stale bread in his lap. A half link of hard, dried sausage that took effort to chew. The price of his loyalty.

Is that all we're worth?

Birgitte's steady chatter hadn't slowed down, and it took him a moment to slip back into the groove of her accent.

"Maybe we'll go to the same school together once they open back up. I don't know if we mean to stay here. Do you have to move out when you lose a war? Or will they let us move back to Essen? It's wonderful there. I had a school and a cat and the people were so much nicer. I had a cat in Schweinfurt too, but *Vati* says it's gone. I think the stories about the Soviets eating cats are fake. They can't be that cruel. They have to be happy the war is ending, too. If we do get to move back home, will you come with us?"

Otto picked at one dry mouthful of the bread. His hands were trembling, the crust crumbling in his grip as he tried to process the dizzying barrage. *The war is over.* He understood the words, but the idea was unfathomable. How could he ever leave?

"Oh hey," she said. "Otto, you don't look so great. Are you feeling okay?"

"I'm fine."

"I know I'm not supposed to be glad he's dead, you should never be glad a person died, but I *want* the war to end," Birgitte confided. "I prayed to be forgiven for being glad. I don't think God can get mad over how you *feel* though, can he? It would be a bit silly when you can't control that. And the war ending is a good thing, isn't it? I can't wait until I can get back to school and my friends and the cinema and Muschi. Muschi is my cat. Did you ever have any pets? You seem like you would like a turtle."

She went on and on, detailing things she remembered. Things she missed. What her life might be. *Their* lives. Each word cut him a little deeper, a sliver closer to bone, until he wanted to grab her by her pretty hair and howl into her face that the bright future she imagined was all a lie. Otto knew better. The golem was right—things never ended. Even death was just one more step in the grim and bitter march. He had read it in the spatters and floorboard stains, the way his old rabbi had told him that heathen shamans read futures in the tattered entrails of disemboweled animals. *You miss your cat? I miss my mom and dad,* Otto wanted to scream at her. *They're gone. Gone forever. Gone for* nothing.

He realized she had gone quiet, watching him. The bread was little more than powder in his hands.

"I guess it's a lot to think about," Birgitte said. "Sorry Otto, I'm just excited. War's been going on so long, I feel like it's been my whole life."

He nodded mutely, did not trust himself to speak.

"Well, it *is* getting late. Goodnight, Otto," she said. She gave him a hug, the part of the night he normally looked forward to all day, but he barely felt it. "I hope you feel better tomorrow. Maybe we can all have dinner together! All of us. Real soon. Wouldn't that just be magical?"

Otto nodded again. Then she shut the door, and he climbed back up into the shadows and wept.

CHAPTER 19

HREE days later, the world caught fire.

Otto woke to the sounds of gunshots, a distant rattle that echoed high above the steepled Prague roofs.

It took him a moment to identify what was happening. At that distance the sound was a pale imitation of the gunfire that had torn apart the attic, that he still sometimes thought he could feel reverberating inside his ears like the trembling whine of some trapped insect burrowing its way in deeper toward his brain. When he focused, he could hear muffled voices, too, yelling among the distant clatter.

He'd heard shooting before, stray singular pops here and there that came from the west—*the Trainyard*—but this time it sounded different. Not the isolated, orderly shots. These fired again and again and again, without stop, and others answered their call in response like the clearing of a massive mechanical throat.

He tried his best to ignore them, but they continued on and on, others sporadically joining in across the city. It didn't matter. It didn't concern him. Whatever was happening wasn't important, he told himself, but he couldn't suppress a light-headed hope that flittered about inside his belly on butterfly wings.

Hitler was dead. If Birgitte was right about that, and right about the war ending… but he didn't allow himself to follow the thought too far. The idea of it was still too much for him to fully consider. Instead, he tried to while away the hours with his usual mundane tasks. None of them yielded much. He couldn't concentrate to read.

The golem still loomed over him, so near completion, but he couldn't bring himself to set the last pieces in place. He might never need to.

The thought had a gravity all of its own.

He wondered what news Birgitte would bring. What food, too. He tried to nap, but couldn't make himself lie still. He considered trying to clean, but that idea seemed even more ludicrous than the others. Instead, he sat beneath the window, looking up at the sky, watching the shifting of the clouds across the great blue wall through the slits in the shutter. With the slats angled upwards, there was nothing else to see and only little of the warmth filtered through. The cloudy days always made it difficult to tell when sunset would come, but he waited and watched just the same as the day dragged onward and he waited and wanted and felt the sturdy roots of hope entangle themselves inside him.

If he hadn't been keeping vigil, he probably wouldn't have seen them.

Twin black flecks against the sky, far away at first but growing. And growing.

Birds, he thought at first, but they weren't moving like birds. They were approaching too quickly, and then they dipped lower toward the rooftops. It occurred to him that they weren't so far off at all, that they were coming closer and closer and swinging in low.

A burst of flame ignited beneath one of the birds that were not birds at all, then a second followed, flashes of light that stabbed at his eyes before the roar reached him. A third blast, much closer. The fourth was only two streets down, and the sound of it wasn't just deafening, it was a physical force that rolled through the walls, through Otto himself. The ground bucked beneath his feet, a massive, furious beast, and then his feet were flailing in the air and he hit the ground. His head bounced against the floorboards and an awful, jagged pain stabbed up into his ribs.

Somewhere, in the back of his mind, a man in a black uniform opened fire on the golem and then Otto's world exploded, too.

Reverberations thrummed in ugly chords through his bones and joints and belly and set his teeth chattering. A whine shrilled through his ears and he tasted iron. He dug around underneath himself until he found what he had landed on—the hand-cranked drill, he noted, the drill bit now damp and smeared in red—and threw it as best he could manage. Then he waited on his hands and knees, gasping and pulling at air that would not come. He'd bitten his lip. Blood and spit drooled down toward the ground, but he couldn't feel much beyond the knifing into his side. Breathing was the important thing. Each attempt brought a tiny shallow burst more than the one before, but it felt like he was sucking his life back into himself through a cracked straw.

A snowstorm of dust spiraled down from the rafters, past where the golem hunched, impervious to the force of the blast. The window, he remembered. The glass. If it broke, then someone would come to replace it. They'd find their way up into the attic and the game would be up. If it broke, all hope was lost. But the window held. The waste bucket had tipped and flooded across the floor in a foul, ghastly smelling wave that he was only beginning to process, but not much other damage had occurred. There wasn't that much to destroy.

He hurt. He wanted to cry, wanted to scream, but the most he could manage was a grunting croak. Someone in the house below was having no such difficulties, was howling, needle-sharp and keening and terrified. Birgitte.

Otto made it as far as the attic door before his better sense caught up with him. She was fine or she wasn't, but there was nothing he could do to help her.

"Birgitte?" Her mother called out. "Birge?"

Otto at last gulped in a proper lungful of air and the hurting in his ribs blossomed into full bloom. He pressed his hand against the white-hot pulse, gritted his teeth and waited for it to stop, but it didn't, and so he pushed the door open just a crack anyway. The door leading out to the hallway was still closed, but he could hear them more clearly, both from his parents' room. Birgitte continued to sob, but the fear had settled into something manageable and her mother shushed her, droned out a steady stream of reassurances.

"Don't worry, Birge. It's going to be fine. We'll hit them back and we'll… we'll be fine. Your father will know what to do. He'll be home soon, okay, Birge?"

Otto imagined Birgitte nodding, her body pressed against her mother's, her mother stroking her hair. An ugly, awful weight of wanting filled his gut. He pressed his forehead against the door, wishing for something, but he wasn't quite sure what he craved, only that it was nowhere to be found hidden in the attic in the unliving dark and the stench of old oil and feces. To be held. To hold. To… something.

He wanted his mother. Such a simple wanting, but it sunk talon and hook and tooth into him, sharper even than the ache in his side, and did not let him go. He pressed his palms to the door and imagined that it was her voice, that she whispered to him and folded him in her arms. For a moment he willed Ilsa to return, just so he wouldn't be so alone.

"What are we going to do?" Birgitte asked.

"We're going to wait until your father gets home," her mother insisted again. "He'll be home any minute. You'll see."

But when nighttime unfurled its wings and made its claim across the wounded city, he hadn't returned and the distant sirens continued to wail. The sporadic drumroll of gunfire answered in turn.

CHAPTER 20

THE night passed, a ponderous funeral march of agonizing minutes and empty hours.

The Man never came home, and Birgitte never brought food. The two never returned downstairs to the kitchen. As best Otto could tell, they must have fallen asleep while huddled together. She'd forgotten him.

Otto waited anyway. Just one more night without food shouldn't have been so hard, but after eating meals again for so many nights, it was somehow even worse. The only thing left of the crackers was dust.

When he snuck out to fill his water cup, he paused for a moment to peer into his parents' old bedroom. The two slumbering shapes were curled up together in one pitifully small huddle. He waited for only a moment before retreating. There was nothing he could offer her. He wasn't really sure why he should want to offer her anything.

At some point he must have closed his eyes as well, because when he startled awake it was daytime and he was still slouched against the piano, completely exposed. That awful sour chalk taste was heavy in his mouth again, but he had nothing to clean it out and so he chewed his tongue until the sapor dulled and he could think. His lip ached where he'd bitten it. His side was a knotted ball of swollen misery.

Birgitte's mother was talking to her, the two of them calling back and forth down the hallway.

"Practical clothes only," her mother said. She said another few words in German that he couldn't decipher. Then she paused and took a deep breath. "The rest we can figure out later."

They were packing. He knew the tone, even if he hadn't recognized all the words. Otto remembered his own mother sounding the same before she brought Otto upstairs to the attic. His stomach throbbed with a deadly hollowness. Not just hunger, but a strangely terrifying weakness. It occurred to him that he could die from not eating. That he was veering dangerously close to the brink of something he couldn't come back from. Breathing took an effort. The slats of his ribs made him think of the golem's stepladder chest. A glance underneath the sleepshirt showed him the violet, violent blossoms of bruises among the thin ridges.

"You said he'd be here. We have to wait for him," Birgitte insisted. She sounded younger than she did during their nighttime conversations, as if the trauma had stripped back the bark of years to some softer interior.

Birgitte's mother was spared an immediate response by the telephone jangling down below. She stomped her way down the stairs, mumbling short, angry words as she went. When she picked the phone off of its cradle, her words garbled into furious squawks.

Otto eased the door open and peeked out into the hallway. Sunlight streamed everywhere, garishly bright, obscene and upsetting. The day leaked into the attic each day too, but in such anemic, thin doses that it was tolerable. This was nearly unbearable. He squinted as he stepped out into the hall.

Into daylight.

He was standing in the hallway of the house, standing upright, during the day. He shook his head in something close to disbelief.

Birgitte's door was open and she scurried around, her arms full of clothes and schoolbooks, piling them into a massive suitcase that was thrown across her bed before stripping them out, reorganizing, and gathering more.

She didn't look up until he was in the doorway. When she saw him, she let out a yelp.

"Otto! You startled me." She pressed a slim hand over her heart, still holding a sleepshirt in her hands, all pretty and clean and pink. "What are you doing down here?"

He picked at his smock, intensely aware of how shabby it looked. The filth and the stains. At night, there was a sort of promise in the gloom that made their conversations feel like an intimate secret just between the two of them. With daylight streaming through the window, it felt crude and clumsy. Magicless. Mechanical. Otto felt a flush creep up his neck.

"I wanted to help. I'm sorry." He wasn't sure why he was apologizing, but he felt it was important that he did.

"Are you okay? I don't know what's going to happen," she said. "Oh! I forgot to bring you food last night."

"It's okay."

"We just finished lunch, but I can see if there is any left over. With the rations, and mom packing, I'm not sure…"

The offer sent a nauseating wave of wanting through him, but he shook his head. "It's okay. Not right now."

"Oh, Otto," she said. "We're leaving. Will you be alright here? Once *Vati* gets home, Mom says we're going. Leaving Prague. Mom said to get ready, that he'll be back any moment. He should've been back already. I wish you could come with us."

Otto had to concentrate on her words to tease the meaning out. She was talking too quickly and the pain in his side made it difficult to focus.

"What if he doesn't come back?" He supposed he meant to assure her, give her some comfort—after all, wasn't that why he'd come down during the daylight hours?—but the words slipped out just the same.

Her mouth opened and stayed that way for a long moment. "Of course he will. Won't he? You don't think… He's my father, Otto. Or… or I guess maybe you want all this to happen?" she gestured at the window, but Otto wasn't sure what she was pointing to. All he saw was an empty sky and the blank façades of empty buildings. "Everyone hates us here. Maybe you do too?"

Otto dropped his gaze back to the clean pink camisole in her hands. The silky shimmer of it. The cleanness. Didn't he want them to suffer? Hadn't he prayed for it, plotted to cut their throats while they slept? Wasn't it good for them to leave, to die, to suffer?

He said nothing, could barely manage a shrug and a shake of his head.

She stamped her foot on the ground. "That's all? How can you not care? My dad could be hurt out there, my mom is in a panic and all you can think about is—"

"They shot my mama in the head," Otto whispered. The words scraped bloody trenches up from his throat, set him trembling as if they had a physical weight that might bend him under. "There's still blood on the mattress where I sleep at night. I watched Papa bleed to death. Right upstairs. Right in front of me. There's a stain where he died. And I… I watched."

His father stared up at him as he cowered inside the belly of the golem. The inventor's eyes were glassy and blank, stripped of love. Of life. And yet, in their final flicker, they sought him out.

The pink camisole. As long as Otto looked at it, he didn't have to see the crime play out in his mind again.

He had watched while they died. Hidden while they paid for his life with their own. He had *allowed* it, and knowing that there was nothing he could have done to stop it or change anything didn't matter because he'd eaten the food Birgitte left out. Because he was standing with sun streaming through the window while she chatted with him, a few steps from where they were murdered. Because he didn't hate her.

Because he hadn't died too.

Every bit of it was a betrayal, and despite all that he still didn't want her father to be dead. He didn't want her to feel that awful hollow weight too. He should be crying, he supposed, but he wasn't.

Birgitte stared at him, eyes wide, her hands covering her mouth.

"I'm so sorry," she said. She reached out to him but whatever she saw in Otto's face made her change her mind.

Otto nodded. Suddenly he didn't want to talk to her anymore. He didn't want to help. He didn't want to see her pretty face or her pretty clothes or all the things she'd taken from him. He was tired. He felt old. The sunlight was all wrong. His thoughts turned muddy in the sun, hadn't he learned that over the last few weeks? He wanted to be back upstairs, in the shadows, in the attic, there alone with the hulking metal god that said nothing. Did nothing. Felt nothing. He'd had enough.

Then the front door crashed open, and chaos poured in.

CHAPTER 21

"**R**ENÉE? Birge?" The Man's voice boomed out, and then Birgitte pushed past Otto, handing him the camisole as she went.

"*Vati!*" she called back.

Otto watched her go. He should slip back up to the attic, he knew. Leave this room that was no longer his own. He should hide in his burrow and wait for whatever was happening to happen. It didn't concern him, did it? When they left, he could go back to hunting for whatever scraps of food. The trash, he supposed. He could find something to eat there. They wouldn't take the trash with them.

He rubbed the soft, clean cloth between his fingers, then tossed it aside. He dropped to his hands and knees and crawled over to the stairwell, to watch through the banister's gap.

Renée came running in from the kitchen but Birgitte got there first, bounded down the last of the stairs and threw her arms around the Man, the momentum carrying them up against the wall. He folded them both in his arms, buried his face against each of their heads, one at a time. He kissed the top of their heads and held them close against him. When he kissed Birgitte's hair, an impossible wave of envy crashed over Otto, something so monstrous it made him dizzy. Not just envy, and certainly not the sadness of the night before. A red-tinged hate that guttered with acidic heat inside his chest.

The perfect little family, standing in the doorway, holding each other close in the same exact spot his own family once had, long before, and never would again. She had pushed past him without a second thought.

When Birgitte's father looked up, most of the feeling passed. Dried blood fanned down one cheek and his neck, soaked the collar of his shirt. Soot and crusted filth caked his face and shoulders, decorated him in reds and blacks like all those terrible parade banners. Something was wrong with one of his ears, Otto noticed, but it wasn't until he traced the smears of blood that he realized it wasn't wrong really, it was simply missing. A mangled lump of tattered flesh, unrecognizable, had replaced it. Otto touched his own ear automatically, tugged at the scabby, scarred lobe.

"Frank? What happened?"

"*Vati*, your ear."

"A bomb hit. Right there by the factory. There were people in the street, a lot of them. I tried to help, but then a second one…" He touched the mess of his ear and grimaced. "It doesn't matter. Get your things. With all the confusion, no one will notice if we slip out. If we're lucky, they'll think I was out in the street too."

Renée gestured toward the three suitcases lined up along the wall.

"We're half packed. Birgitte?"

"I'll go finish," she said. She dashed up the stairs two at a time and shot right past Otto. She didn't look down as she rushed by.

"Good," Birgitte's father said, looking toward the suitcases. "This is good. Ten minutes and we're gone."

Renée placed a gentle hand against the side of his face.

"How badly are you hurt?"

He shook his head instead of responding.

"Do you think we'd be safer if we stayed? I want to go too, but if the Russians are dropping bombs in the streets, if there's shooting going on…"

"Renée, those bombers weren't Russian."

"I don't understand," she said. "The British?"

"No." He ran a hand across his scalp, winced, and checked his hand. Otto caught a glimpse of fresh, wet red. He wiped it on his pants, studied the print as he spoke. "Those bombers were German. There was some… some riot. The streets were full of people yelling in Czech, waving flags. They weren't just rioting, they were coming for *us*. For the factory. Christoph is dead. Someone started shooting." he shook his head in disbelief. "The police got it under control, but the street was still full when the first bomb hit. Packed full, shoulder to shoulder. A German plane dropped the bomb."

"Are you sure?"

"You know what I make at that factory, Renée. I know a German bomber when I see one. That means one thing. We need to go now. Before anyone notices I'm missing. Pack food, anything essential. Whatever we can bring, everything else we'll just leave behind. Ten minutes. Five is better. We'll get a car or we'll walk. We can figure it out as we go."

Renée nodded, headed back to the kitchen. The Man waited until she was out of sight before he sagged against the wall, rubbed at his eyes with filthy fingers. He shook his head at some internal monologue or memory or in simple disbelief. He moved stiffy, wearily, his head bowed from the weight of it all as he shuffled over to the small closet before the doorway. In he went.

Ten minutes. In ten minutes, the house would be Otto's again. The idea seemed impossible. German planes bombing a German-held city? Riots in the streets? He wondered what old Ms. Fena thought now, and what flag she was waving. If she was dead.

A moment later, Birgitte's father reemerged from the closet.

In his hands, he held a gun.

Otto stared. He'd never thought to check the closet since they moved back in. It seemed ludicrous that he hadn't, but it never even occurred to him. He could have had a gun. Then a follow-up, uglier thought tagged along: it didn't matter if he had a gun. Gun or knife or golem, the weak point was *him*, not his tools.

The man examined the pistol. An odd-looking, boxy thing with a handle like a wooden knob. It looked like a toy, bolted together. The man fed the stick holding the bullets in near the front of the gun, and then he tucked it, muzzle down, into the back of his pants. He tugged the jacket of his uniform over top of it to keep it out of sight.

"Is it that bad?" Renée asked. She stood in the doorway, watching him.

"It's bad," he said. "But we'll be fine as long as—"

A fist pounded on the door.

CHAPTER 22

"**Y**OU have to stop them," Renée said. "Don't let them in here."

The Man brushed his hands across his uniform, reached out and pushed the door open. The outside sirens wailed louder for a moment and three men stepped in. From his vantage point, Otto could not see up to their faces, could only see a part of their uniforms—two wore gray pants tucked into their boots, one wore black. The door settled behind them.

"*Obermeister* Frank Van Meter?" the man in black asked, his voice sharp and clipped and clear. He sounded genuinely surprised. "An unexpected pleasure."

"*Hauptstumführer*. I'm afraid I don't know your name." Birgitte's father's hand strayed toward the back of his pants where the butt of the pistol protruded. "What brings you here?"

The man in black stepped forward and her father retreated a step. The jacket was decorated in silver, his arm circled in a red band. A low, sickly throbbing began to press against the back of Otto's eyes. "We came to make sure your family was safe. We look after our own. I was told you were on duty."

"I finished for the day," he said. "I went home."

"So I see." The man in black turned to the two men with him, gestured, and they headed out into the street. He did not continue until the door settled closed once more. "Bad business, today. I trust the damages aren't going to cause any delays?"

"Nothing that we can't handle, *Hauptstumführer*."

Another step in, another step yielded. Otto could see higher now, almost to his face, but with the foyer light now behind him and the hat angled low, it might as well have been carved out of night. Otto shrank back.

"That's a good thing. And your injuries?"

"I can handle those, too."

"Good. Good," he said again. This time he only advanced a half step. Birgitte's father backpedaled the full pace, pressed himself against the wall across from the luggage. "You are staying here with your wife and daughter, yes?"

Otto resisted the urge to crawl back towards safety, instead settled himself until his cheek pressed against the ground. He was visible, he knew. Not easily, but he could see her father's face, which meant her father only had to look up to see Otto. Nonetheless, he stayed, could not bring himself to move.

"Yes, sir. My daughter is upstairs, my wife is in the kitchen. I've been away for two days now, and I'd like to spend some time with them. What can I do to help you so you can get back on your way?"

The man in black ignored the question.

"That's a good thing. Family is a blessing." He paused for a long moment before pointing one long finger toward the suitcases that lined the front hall. "But abandoning your duty? That would be something else entirely."

Birgitte's father was silent. Otto realized the entire house was, that in the kitchen Renée had stopped rummaging around and even Birgitte seemed to pause in her efforts. Not the same lonely silence that the house had held when he crept, alone, through the dark. This was a living, vibrating thing, a hulking presence with a sinister smile. Otto drew in a breath and held it, too frightened to exhale.

Birgitte's father flexed his fingers at his waist, hooked his thumbs up under his belt, a matter of inches from where Otto knew the handle of the pistol was pressing into his back.

Do it, Otto silently urged. *It's just the one, right now. Take the gun before the others get back. Kill. Let every trace of him be forever erased. Yimakh shemo.*

"I—" he began, but the man in black cut him off.

"The riot today rattled you." He did not ask it as a question, and he did not wait for Birgitte's father to reply. "It was an ugly thing. But war is an ugly thing. Our enemies get closer. People are afraid. They say things, they worry. They doubt. But what they don't seem to realize is that more and more Soviets are defecting to us with every passing day. They'd rather join our cause than fight it. The Western forces have slowed their advance. We stand on the edge of a razor. Tiny things can push that balance one way or another. Even a single person, perhaps." He paused, as if to consider, but Otto had the impression that the conversation had been carefully steered to this point, that there was no consideration left. Only inevitability. "Even you."

Birgitte's father cleared his throat. "*Hauptstumführer*, I am—we are—happy to do anything we can."

"It is important that you are. You won't disappoint us, will you, Herr Van Meter?"

"No." The big man's voice was quiet. He clasped his hands in front of himself in unmistakable contrition.

"See to it that you do not. You come highly recommended. You have a lovely family. A lovely house, now that we've cleaned it out. But this city is full of so many... rats."

Otto's headache came on in earnest, a sharp-clawed, dizzying pulse that scraped at the inside of his skull and set his vision swimming along the edges. He allowed himself a short rush of breath, in and out, stolen through clenched teeth.

"Rats?"

"Indeed. Rats living in the walls, chewing away at any loose scraps they can find. Hoping to see us fail. To see us weakened. You know of Reinhard Heydrich, yes?"

"Yes, *Hauptstumführer*."

The shadow of the man shook his head as if to refuse the answer.

"He was more than a man. He was... he was the architect of all of this. Of the cleansing. The Führer called him the man with the iron heart. Isn't that something? I like the sound of it. I was with him, served a year as *Einsatzgruppen*, and then we came here. He led us to search through this city, house by house. Those cowards murdered him for it. Those little Czech rats. But what he built didn't die with him. We have many enemies, and loyalty is a strange thing. The people of this city are vermin, but not you. You are loyal, yes? Heydrich may be gone, the Führer may be gone, but not you. And not me. Not for a very long time, I think. We've got miles left to go and these factories will continue to run, *Obermeister*."

Any humor had left his voice.

"Can..." Birgitte's father swallowed. "Can I get you a drink?"

"I don't drink, Herr Van Meter. I'm on duty."

"If you don't drink, what's your vice?"

The man in black hesitated for a moment and Otto got the impression something important was being said or implied, but he couldn't quite figure out what. "Well, now. I smoke?"

The color drained out of Otto's world.

A man, dressed in black, standing over him. Standing with his feet planted in a fresh pool of blood. A cigarette smoldered in his hand.

The Man offered him something. A promise of cigarettes, cigars, Otto wasn't certain because he couldn't hear clearly over his pounding heart. Over the sound of thunder and gears that rolled through his chest.

It was him. *Him*. Otto was sure of it. It didn't matter how he knew, it didn't matter that it made little sense. The killer had come back.

He was going to get the knife, march down there, and... a hand settled gently on his shoulder.

He turned and Ilsa was there beside him.

He had strayed from the attic during the day, had forgotten the ghosts, ignored them, managed to pretend they weren't there, but they were. Were there, were always there, would always be there. A scream built up in his chest, threatened to tear its way out of him, but she raised a finger to her lips, and all at once, he could feel it again: his mother's hand mashing against his mouth, the stink of her sweat, the way his lips bled. The ruined face as her head came apart. The sound died inside him.

The face of his murdered mother stared back at him, terrible to see, but then it shifted into the kindly face of the older woman from Birgitte's room…

…and then the house was empty. No men casually bantered about life and death and rats and cruel designs. The doorway was different. Glass panels on either side of the door threw squares of glowing sun onto either side of a neat, carefully selected little floral rug. The way leading into the study was wider. The wooden floor seemed brighter. Cleaner. All the stains and boot prints had been scrubbed out.

The white-haired woman winced as she sat down beside him. The smell of lavender hung around her in a halo, and he breathed in deeply as she stroked his hair.

"You're going to be okay. Relax, Otto. Breathe. It's going to be alright."

Otto nodded. His knees hurt, he realized. He wondered how long he had been sprawled out on the ground, looking down into the front foyer where no one stood. Only sunlight. He tried to brace his hands underneath himself to push himself upright, but he realized his strength was gone. That his body felt weak, pained, stripped to its barest foundation.

"You're Ilsa, aren't you?" he asked, and she nodded, smiled at him. "What's going on? Are you… this is your old house, isn't it? You used to live here a long time ago. Before the war. Didn't you?"

It was the only explanation he could think of, the only thought that tied it all into any sensical pattern. She was some long-gone relative, reaching out from beyond the grave to help him. And, oddly, he realized he wasn't afraid anymore. He could have kissed her.

A tear trickled down the lines of her cheek, her smile turning terribly sad. Her lower lip trembled, although it might have been her age as much as emotion. She was old. Far older than his mother had ever managed. Far older than he would, probably.

"Oh, Otto. No, dear." She paused, took his hand in hers. Her skin was warm against his own, dry as crisp autumn leaves and yet still gentle. Still soft. As he watched, her age leeched into him, prowled with age-spot footprints as it advanced up his arms. His fingers were bony and swollen, gnarled, the nails yellowed and chipped. His hands trembled of their own accord. Veins laced across the jutting bone, protruding blue wires beneath thin skin. His wrist had a series of fresh thin cuts along the back of it, a thick white scar along his palm. He marveled at the sight.

"But..."

"I didn't live here, Otto." She squeezed his hand. "You did."

Then she was gone and he was alone, looking down upon the two men. The smell of lavender faded, slipped beneath the tobacco smoke trailing thin threads from the cigarette in the hands of the man in the black uniform.

The ghost was gone, but he could still feel the memory of her hand gripping his, keeping him from rising, from moving. A deep breath in, a deep breath out. Just the way his mother used to comfort him.

The man below pointed to Birgitte's father with the smoldering cigarette. Otto wasn't sure when he had lit it.

"As I said, you come highly recommended, so we are willing to overlook this... moment of doubt. We have the utmost faith in you. And in the country. This war isn't lost, you know. Think about the world you want waiting for you on the far side of war. We'll keep your family safe, but don't let them be the barrier that keeps you from your duty. For all of our sakes."

"Understood, *Hauptstumführer*."

The door behind the man swung open and he raised his hand in salute, waited until Birgitte's father returned it. The fingers of his shadow stretched their way up, stair after stair, until they nearly brushed against Otto's own hand.

"Herr Van Meter," the man in the black uniform said. Then he stepped out the door and closed it behind him and he was gone.

A moment later, Renée came spilling in from the kitchen, her hand clasped over her mouth in an almost identical gesture to the one Otto had seen from Birgitte when he told her how his parents died.

"Oh, Frank. But we still have to risk it, it's not too late…"

Birgitte's father shook his head, waved her away. He locked the front door, took a deep breath, and his shoulders slumped. He gave a long look at the suitcases.

"Put it back, Renée."

"Frank—"

"All of it. Put it back. We're not going anywhere. We're staying."

CHAPTER 23

OTTO retreated to the attic.

The flurry of activity below had stopped, the energy had deflated, and the rasp of suitcases dragged back to the rooms where they'd been packed sounded far too similar to the thud of bodies being dragged down the stairs. More than anything, he felt numb.

I didn't live here, Otto. You did.

Ilsa, her face complete, with her arm around him. His hands withered, old, scarred. The smell of lavender.

He inspected his hands. An eight-year-old's dirty hands, not scarred. No frailty beyond skeletal thinness. They looked correct, didn't they?

His head hurt. In the dim light it was hard to see, but he imagined bloodstains all down the stairwell, that he crawled across ragged red lumps of corpses as he fought his way up to the attic, twisted fingers clutching toward him, broken knees and jutting bones on proud display as he dragged himself toward the golem's lair. The sour chalk taste was back, and he was hungry. Oh so hungry.

He hunted through the bags for any scraps he might have overlooked but found none. He crawled across the ground, nose low, hoping to spot some crumbs, and when he at last found a small pile beside the golem's feet he shoveled it into his mouth without hesitation before he identified the gritty, tasteless scrape on his gums. Sawdust left over from drilling or knocked loose by the bombing. He swallowed instead of spitting it out.

"Mama?" he croaked into the speaker box. "Papa?"

No response.

He sat with it in his lap, waiting to hear if it would talk to him, mock him, threaten him, but it was just a scrap of hole-punched metal. It wasn't as heavy as it looked. Just a shell, really. The mask beside it watched him with brass-rimmed goggles. The open slot of a mouth gaped. Twin bullet holes had broken the word written upon the brow. He fished the screwdriver out of the toolbox and scratched out the damaged letter, etched it in the steel above in his own clumsy handwriting. By the time he was done, his wrists ached and the tip of the screwdriver was bent. It wasn't pretty, but nothing in his father's notes said it needed to be. All that was left was to carry the face up and bolt it into place. But to what end? The golem wouldn't ease the hurt in his stomach, would it?

He polished the steel with one filthy sleeve until it shone.

Dinnertime arrived—Renée called out as she did every night, but with none of her usual enthusiasm—and Birgitte headed down. Otto followed, a few minutes later. He couldn't help himself. The rattle of pots and pans called him as surely as if they were a summoning. The pain of hunger was just too much. He left the knife tucked under his mattress. He couldn't imagine much use for it. It wouldn't keep Ilsa or the man in the black uniform away, and he couldn't muster much fear of the family below.

Down the hallway once more and back to her bedroom where her suitcase slumped, half unpacked, in a drift of clothes. There was no tidiness, no urgency. It looked like surrender. Otto picked his way across the mess, over to the hole.

The Man sat at the table as usual, but this time he didn't bother with a newspaper. Renée brought in their three bowls and set them at their places in silence. Her hair was a mess, her pretty white dress wrinkled and disheveled. Each bowl had a pair of tiny, shriveled dumplings and a thin slice of bread. The broth was mostly clear. When they ate, the clack of spoons on porcelain made up the majority of their conversation.

Otto watched them, counting time by the spoonful. Birgitte ate one of her two dumplings, and then started on the next. *Stop,* he begged her. *Please.* But of course she didn't hear, didn't hesitate, didn't even slow down. She was going to gobble it all up and leave nothing, she was going to forget him again, and he'd have to crawl back upstairs and make it through the night on a fistful more of sawdust. A mewling whimper crept up his throat. The crust of bread remained on her plate. Maybe he would get the crust. Birgitte touched it with one finger, tested the firmness, but she didn't eat. Just rested her finger there, considering.

By the time Renée spoke, Otto was sweating.

"I still think we should try."

"We're not leaving," her husband answered.

"But—"

"No, Renée. If we go, they'll find us."

"You said—"

"I know what I said, but the camps are real. And they would do it without a second thought, if they didn't just line us up in front of the wall. You've seen the bodies. I'm too important for them to let slip away. If I step out of line, they'll make an example out of me. Out of us. We keep from doing anything that will give them a reason to hurt us. Anything at all."

Birgitte's mother set down her fork, watched her husband over steepled fingers. "What about Birge?"

"What about me?" Birgitte asked.

Her parents ignored her.

Her father shook his head slowly. "I don't know. Maybe, if we sent her away alone. But not you, and not me. And where would she go? You want our daughter alone out there?"

"What about me?" Birgitte asked again.

Her mother seemed to deflate. "I don't... I don't know. Nothing, dear." She stared down at her bowl. She'd eaten only one of the meager, shriveled dumplings. After a moment she offered her daughter a pitiful attempt at a smile. "Are you still hungry?"

Birgitte looked back and forth between her two parents. "Is there more to eat?"

"Renée —" her father began, but Renée shook her head, pushed herself to her feet.

"You can have mine, Birge. I'm not all that hungry tonight," she said. She swapped her plate out with Birgitte's and headed to the kitchen, dish in hand.

Birgitte's father watched her go, his eyes damp and an expression on his face that reminded Otto so strongly of how his father had looked at his mother that it caused a physical pain in his chest.

Love. A look of love.

Otto realized the mistake he'd made. Since they walked through the door, Otto had thought of him as the Man, a mindless, murderous monster, but that was all wrong. He served a monstrous cause, but he was so many things beyond that too. He had fears. He loved. He was a father, a husband, and countless other things. He wasn't the one who had killed Otto's parents. He hadn't been the one laughing over their bodies. He was simply a man, shaking his head in defiance of the bell chime.

Otto wished he had killed him before he ever knew.

Frank turned to his daughter, the same helpless, unguarded look on his face, and then he frowned.

Birgitte had picked up her mother's dumpling and set it in the center of her napkin, and the slice of bread on top of it.

A pit opened in Otto's stomach, a black, devouring thing that left him dizzy with dread. The warm thoughts about common humanity evaporated in an instant. Every other meal, Frank had ignored her, but now he watched with furrowed brow as she folded the napkin gently over the meal and tucked the corners into itself. A pretty packet of food. A gift. She didn't look up, didn't see his curiosity, didn't notice how obvious her plans were. How with each delicate fold, she incriminated herself. Why else would she steal food, pack it up like a gift, except to give it to someone? Otto bit against his lip to keep himself from whimpering, from shouting out for her to stop, from making any sound at all.

Just eat the damn food. I can wait. I've been hungry enough times before.

"Please..." Otto whispered against the floorboards. He wasn't sure if he was praying to Birgitte or to God.

A slow disbelief dawned across her father's face.

"Rats in the walls," he said to no one in particular. "My knife. Mice. Birge, what are you doing?"

She flinched, looked up at him, her blue eyes wide and terrified. For a moment Otto managed to fool himself into thinking she could sell the lie, wished with all his might she could think of some reason for why she was preparing a gift with no one to give to. "I... I..." A flush crept up from her neck, her stammer as incriminating as the packet in her hands. "I'm sorry..."

"Renée! Get in here. Birge, what have you done?"

CHAPTER 24

OTTO sprinted down the hallway as the table erupted into bellows below.

"*Vati*, no—"

"Frank?"

"Where are they? How many of them? *Mein Gott...*"

Otto passed through the library in three steps, had the bookshelf door open and shut and locked a moment later, even before the distant scrape of furniture against floorboards announced that they were coming, and in a hurry. He clamored up the staircase on all fours. He looked around, tried for some way out, some escape, some way to fight.

The knife.

He dug it out from beneath the filthy mattress, hefted it in his hand. The weight of it that had seemed so solid and impressive at midnight now felt flimsy. Impotent. He tried to imagine racing back downstairs to confront Birgitte's father, but the idea was laughable. The man was three times his size, made of muscle and desperation, and Otto's righteous indignation seemed so much less impressive of a force when the man could fight back.

And he had the gun.

Otto could picture the box-framed pistol with the strange handle knob. He was willing to bet Frank had never returned it to the closet. It was still tucked into the waist of his pants. Even if there was some chance that Otto's knife was enough to make him match up against Frank, the gun decided it. There was only one thing to do.

He set to work.

He was close, so close, only the last few pieces needed their place.

He reached for the toolbox, but in his hurry, he sent it tipping over. It crashed against the floor. He held his breath for a moment before realizing it didn't matter whether they heard it or not. There was no time to wait. He crawled on his hands and knees, groping in the dim twilight for the screwdriver.

The sound of arguing voices swelled. *They're coming,* Otto thought, his mind turning it into a sing-song sort of rhythm. *They're coming. They're coming. They're coming.* Closer and closer, their words becoming clearer as they neared, Birgitte's father's deep baritone rising above the rest.

"They'll kill us, don't you understand? They'll kill us all!"

The sound of a slap. Not a light, chiding cuff, but a swing with weight behind it. Birgitte's mother let out a choked cry, but did not protest. Birgitte wailed. The slap again, louder.

"Do you think this is a game? Your mother. You. Me. All of us! You know what they do in those camps to people who have been helping *them* out? You know what they do to the girls there?"

They were in the library.

Otto's hand landed on the screwdriver. He scurried back to the metal face and the speaker box and set it into place over the mouth slot. He had to grip the screws with both hands to keep himself steady enough for them to bite into their grooves.

"Here? In here…?"

Birgitte was sobbing. The voices were quieter now, no more slaps. No more bellows. Something crashed into the bookshelf below.

The screws tightened smoothly, mercifully, without a fight. The final piece would be getting the mask up and onto the head. The copper base jutted up from the neck, but no face. It needed a face.

Otto gripped the polished steel mask, arms straining from the weight as he scrabbled upwards, up over jagged edges and bent joints, his feet struggling to find purchase until he at last reached the ladder. The wooden rungs had a strange, alien warmth to them, completely at odds with the cold metal. His side throbbed. He dragged himself to the top, hooked his elbow over the ladder and heaved the mask up onto the base. It slid into place, and he anchored it with a bolt at the neck and one at the top of the head, just above the word that had been etched into its brow.

He fished a match—one of the last two—from his pocket and struck it, looked into the creation's flat, empty face in the brief flare of light. The brass-rimmed goggles, the lenses smoky black. The speaker-box mouth. The letters clawed into its steel brow among the bullet holes. The match dropped from Otto's fingers and fizzled out long before it hit the floor, but it didn't matter. He'd seen enough to know that his job was complete.

The bookshelf crashed to the floor, took the door with it. Light from below spilled upwards. Otto fought off the desire to scurry for a dark corner.

"Wake up," he whispered to the golem, but it did not move. And it shouldn't, he realized. He was still missing one final piece. The switch that ignited the flame. He thought back to that awful night, the fist clenching in a pool of blood, and suddenly he understood.

Otto fished the knife from his toolbelt, gripped it by the blade, and dragged it downward. It slit through the meat of his palm without any resistance, could as easily have been sliding through water as it divided his hand open and a red sea spilled forth. He raised his hand and smeared it across the golem's face, below the inscription.

Emét.

Truth. And truth was only one tiny step away from death.

The lamp set into the golem's chest sparked, glinted and gleamed. Something whirred inside the great machine, and with the onerous groan of overburdened hinges and bending metal, it rose. Otto tumbled down onto his back and lay beneath it, looking up, as the footsteps paraded up the stairs. Birgitte was sobbing, begging. Renée hushed her. Frank said nothing at all. His silhouette led the way.

A flashlight clicked on, traced a circle of daylight radiance across the rafters and walls and the floorboards where Otto's family had once lain. Across the rat feces and scraps, filth and oil, and onto the glint of steel. A metal boot, formed from a span of railroad track, bent and welded into submission. A leg, the plated knee hinged with bolts and reinforced with a scrap of bent pipe. The lamp heart that guttered, pale and yellow and ugly. A face painted in blood.

Birgitte's father stood before Otto without seeing him, gun in one hand and flashlight in the other, staring up in slack-jawed awe at the metal man. The other two huddled behind him.

The golem stayed frozen in place.

It hadn't been given a command.

Otto closed his eyes, squeezed them shut as tight as he could and whispered the words like a prayer, the only words he had left. The only command he knew, without his father there to teach him others. The final lesson he had learned before they stole the rest away.

"*Yimakh shemo.*"

CHAPTER 25

THE golem's hand shot out.

Steel fingers folded around Frank's face and the metal creature heaved him up into the air. The gun went off, a bullet whipped past Otto's head and chewed into the rafters, but then the weapon clattered to the ground and the man let out a howl of terror that climbed, climbed, climbed into a girlishly high octave of pain. Frank beat at the metal fist that gripped him, hands of flesh and bone battering and breaking against unyielding, painless steel. His feet drummed against the ribcage, splintered the slats of the stepladder, banged off the metal sheets and the cogs and gears that Otto had not yet concealed. The golem rose up to its full height, tall enough that the goggles it wore for eyes nearly scraped the highest peak of the rafters. The lamp inside its chest flickered and blazed brighter, lit the room up in slashes of light and crazed shadow, streaks of absolutes, a flash of lightning that would not fade. Frank's wheeling arms formed a strobing blur of dark behind him, a roulette wheel of light and black.

"*Vati!*" Birgitte screamed.

The golem squeezed.

The squeal of pain cut off immediately. One moment Birgitte's father was struggling, shrieking, his hopeless battle illuminated in the electric glow; the next he was limp.

"Don't look," Renée said. She pulled Birgitte to her chest. "Frank!"

The golem opened its fist and the Man dropped, his head deflated. He may have been looking upwards, but Otto couldn't be sure. There was no face left. No eyes, no nose. No stern, furrowed brow. All of it had been reduced to soggy mulch. An obscene bubble passed through what might have been his mouth, his life a red balloon slipping past ruined lips, swelling and bursting across his ruined uniform.

Strange, thick jelly dripped in pink globs from the golem's fingers and slopped to the floor.

Otto marveled at the monstrosity above him. At the sheer, terrifying weight of it. He had built it from scraps, woven it together, bent the metal and fit the pieces together, all those little hatreds and fears and wrongs committed against him, but he'd had no appreciation for it as a whole. He had seen it in pieces so long that he had forgotten what it was he was building. The size. The unyielding glint of metal. He'd had no appreciation for what it could manage, for what *he* could manage. He stared in awe at the simple, violent monstrosity and wondered if God had felt the same in Eden, standing before his rutting beast made of rust-colored clay, powerless to control it beyond the façade of ownership.

Kill, he had said, and it had killed. *Let even their names be erased.*

He felt—once more, and clearer than ever before—like an old man watching the scene play its course, a scene he had witnessed countless times before. The whole awful history of man laid out in grim relief: the brainless monster towering above the naïve boy who had created it, but did not know the words to calm its rage. To stop it. To take it all back.

Then Renée pushed her daughter toward the stairwell and stumbled forward. She hit the floor, feet sliding in the blood and muck, and when she rose with red-stained knees on her pretty white dress, she held the gun in her hand. Birgitte's mother stood her ground and raised the weapon. Not aiming at the golem.

Aiming at Otto.

The golem reached her first.

A casual backhand and Otto heard the grinding wet snap of bone pulverizing. The Woman flopped against the wall and slid down. Jagged bits of her ribs poked out at pointed angles from inside her dress. Her eyes bulged, sightlessly rolling as she slid down.

Birgitte let out a wordless, helpless keen of terror, fingernails raking into her own face. She turned and ran.

The golem followed.

"No!" Otto screamed. "Stop, let her go!"

The Girl was halfway down the stairs when it caught her. She never stood a chance.

He didn't see it happen, but he could hear it.

Could hear the music of her voice cut off. The heavy drumbeat thunder as it struck her again and again, a rolling heartbeat that drowned out his own.

It was over in a moment.

And then there was stillness. Silence reigned, aside from the wet dripping sound and the sirens outside.

An hour passed, and then another, but there was no tolling of bells to announce it. The skyline was smeared in pillars of smoke. The Orloj was in flames.

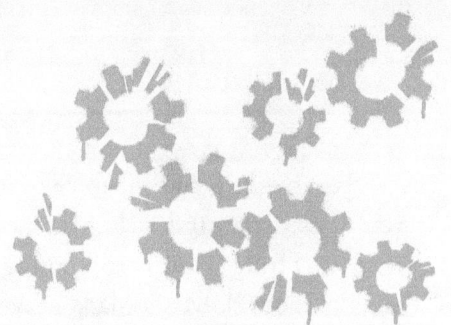

CHAPTER 26

H E opened his eyes.

It was all a dream, he told himself, as he studied the blood on the attic floor. His father's blood, not hers. His mother's. If he were to look down the awful stairwell, he wouldn't find her body. He would find his own, gunned down by the men who came that first terrible night. He was simply a ghost, haunting without understanding.

It wasn't her life that had been forfeit. It was his own.

The golem towered over him, its fists smeared the color of rust, the flat, empty goggles returning nothing but the dull glint of the dawn's first light. The blood he'd painted across its face to grant it life had dried into a thin, flaking brown ribbon, but there were other marks on its face, other handprints stamped in various stages of freshness. The glint of metal reflected his face back, warped in its proportions and the last comforts of illusion crumbled. An old man's face. A wrinkled, withered visage, eroded by the passing of time. His skin hung loosely. His neck wobbled when he swallowed.

But in some way, he had known that was what he'd find.

Out beyond the window, planes sliced across the open blue sky. Not war planes. The gentle contrails of commercial jumbo jets. In the distance, the Orloj chimed its mechanical defiance of death. They'd rebuilt it, he remembered, but he wasn't certain when. He wasn't certain if it had been so damaged that they replaced it with an imitation, or if any scrap of the original remained.

He coughed, and the force of it set his frail body trembling. He was dressed only in his sleep clothes and a threadbare bathrobe, but that felt fitting. He'd been wearing pajamas when he built it, after all. The robe's sleeve was dark, heavy and gummy with blood, and he peeled it back to touch an open wound along the back of his arm. He felt little pain despite the reddened open mouth in the sagging skin that crisscrossed so many other scars. Some were freshly scabbed over. Some were ancient. The blood was still sticky on his withered palm.

Old.

He'd been so young, back then. He'd been just a boy.

After the Van Meters were gone, Otto had waited for the man to come back, that monster in a black uniform. When he returned, Otto would speak the phrase again and that would be that. Maybe, just maybe, it would bring him one step closer to retrieving what had been stolen from him.

But the man never did.

Otto survived the next week off of the Van Meters' packed-up rations and by then a new parade had rolled into town, the old flags torn down and replaced. That was eighty-some years gone by. The man with fire inside him was dead, Otto supposed. Maybe from execution. Maybe simply from old age. After death, the how never really mattered. There was no solace in the pain of a corpse.

The Russian occupation was hard. He was still only a child. He found help in one of his parents' friends from the synagogue, a man who had once been wideset and sweaty and brought food to houses where Jewish families hid. He was skinny now and had a number tattooed on his arm, but his laughter survived and so did his daughter, who smelled like lavender. Her name was Ilsa and a decade later, Otto's mother's wedding ring looked natural on her finger.

Otto felt himself smiling, ran his hands through his wisp-thin hair.

He'd kept the house. He sealed the attic, tended it like a secret garden. Some things weren't meant to be told. When the roof needed repairs, he climbed up that ladder. When Ilsa asked him how he had survived, when she asked about the local rumors of the massacre that left three mangled corpses strewn in the street out front, he'd never been able to answer her. When she wanted to redecorate the library, he'd refused. Little by little, she'd managed to accept his secrets. Little by little, he'd managed to almost forget them.

He'd laughed at his wedding, danced and shattered glass and sang out his joy. He'd worked hard at the Praga factory, piecing together motorcycles and trucks and children's bicycles for decades. The money was good and he'd always had a knack with it, and it brought him a quiet sort of peace. He'd held her in his arms after the miscarriage, when her body shook and she sobbed, and it had torn his heart too, but there was a beauty even in that agony. In holding her. In living a good life. A good man's life.

The smile faded.

The first time he fell, it was in that same library. She had been sitting at the piano, her fingers lazily dancing over the keys, when the world turned dark around the edges and then she was rushing toward him. A moment later, she was dabbing at a gash along his scalp, her fingers pressing against his wrist to check his pulse.

"Just clumsy," she assured him. "You just need some rest."

But for a moment, as she rushed toward him, he'd almost not been able to recognize her.

Little things happened, too. He started looking for any excuse to avoid going outside. The open sky frightened him. Sounds seemed louder. He forgot to eat dinner as often as not, unless Ilsa sat with him and watched over him. Sometimes he found himself unscrewing table legs or hoarding matches, but he wasn't quite sure why.

The doctors called it acute onset of dementia. Warned that he could experience sundowning, that his memories would grow worse at night. That he might remember some parts but forget others. They asked him if his parents had it, but how could Otto know? They never had the chance. The pills they gave him were hard to swallow, harder to keep down, and they tasted like sour chalk coming up. And things got worse.

He'd find himself crouched in closets or in the pantry, cringing away from the sound of her approach. She pretended like it was a game, at first, and would walk through the house calling out his name. Later, she would search in earnest, would find him trembling in the dark where he'd hidden for hours, his legs wet and stinking of urine. Would crawl underneath the bed with him and hold his hand until the horrors passed.

Found you.

"We can handle it," she said. Her beautiful hair had turned the color of smoke. Her face looked hungry, her eyes sunken and neck frail. It was as if his memories were something toxic bleeding into her, sawing the years and pounds from her.

Otto agreed. But he never told her where he disappeared to, when he started vanishing for days at a stretch. He never told her what he worked on. He never told her about the night he found himself standing over her while she slept, a knife in his hand.

He didn't dare.

I didn't live here, Otto. You did.

"Oh Ilsa," Otto whispered. His words wavered as they formed. But he had a hard time picturing her face. It was all slipping away again. So soon. Too soon.

His head hurt. It used to wait longer, didn't it? It used to be just at night when time unweaved and he was dragged back to that moment. Today, it was barely past dawn. Soon, there'd be no safety left at all. Nowhere to run. His hands looked young, for a moment, the scars slithering back into younger, softer skin.

"Please," he whispered, his voice cracking and frail. "I don't want to remember. Not again."

The stench of smoke. The marching boots. The sounds of gun-fire and bombs and the screams. Her screams. How many times had he relived that awful night? Those awful weeks? That terrible final moment with its terrible final command?

There was no ghost back then, of course. Just the imagination of an eight-year-old boy, traumatized and terrified. He understood that. When he was a child, he'd hidden from shadows, from an imagined man hunting him, from the neighbor, from the world itself. But how many times had he paced the halls with Ilsa searching for him, the memories woven inextricable from the present fog? How many times had he played it out again and again in his delirium, those awful words on his lips?

And how many times had the golem stirred?

A low, broken moan escaped him.

"Ilsa…"

If she goes up there, she'll die.

The blood was fresh.

The stairwell yawned behind him, but he was suddenly afraid to look. He'd spent his whole life looking down the barrel of that battered, bloody series of steps, but the thought of looking now…

He turned instead to the golem, restored to its grandeur during those midnight fumblings, impervious to the years. His real father. The father of steel. The creature simply stood waiting, untiring, unquestioning. Unending.

An abomination.

"Why would you hurt her?"

The golem only knew how to obey. That was the way of terrible things. The blood smeared across its face was his own.

"Why won't you die?" he asked.

But he knew that answer, too—it couldn't. Because he had never let it die. After the war, he had told himself he might need it again. When Soviet tanks rolled in decades later, he clung to it. The years rolled by and he never could let go. They'd put something in him, that awful night when he was eight years old. They'd stamped it into the soil of his heart with their boots and he'd let it grow so that it would keep him alive. He'd kept it caged and tame, but terrible things could only be contained so long.

His mother had said to put it to death, and instead he had simply hidden it away. How could he kill the thing that had saved him? Even knowing what it was capable of doing?

"I didn't know how," he whispered. But that wasn't true. He remembered the lesson from so long ago.

The lamp inside the golem's chest glowed, and Otto found himself staring up into it, drowsy, some helpless animal caught in the soporific lure of a predator. He was tired. He wanted to rest. To close his eyes.

He could simply slip back under and forget. Struggling was a choice. He could accept that he was still that terrified boy and never let go. He looked instead to his feet, traced the shadowy blur of shapes until he found it among the clots of spiderwebs and dust and threadbare cloth. The screwdriver, its tip half bent. He tucked it into his pocket.

Then he made his way to the golem and began to climb.

His limbs lacked the nimble, near-inexhaustible energy of youth, but he did not allow himself to hesitate at the jut of pain that sprang through his arms as he dragged himself upward, first onto the knee and then to the ladder. The light blazed above him as his feet scrambled for purchase. Nails snagged at his scrawny legs, metal edges and splintered wood scraped trenches through his skin. His feet slipped, but he held on.

And up he climbed, up into the full blast of the light and beyond, to look into the face of the thing above. The golem waited, unflinching as he traced his trembling fingers across the monstrous, bloody face. The voice box. The goggles, their lenses faded by age into black cataracts. Up to the word written on its brow, half in his father's hand and finished in a child's scrawl.

It did not struggle as he groped in his pocket, set the screwdriver against that first letter.

Otto blinked back tears as he dragged the screwdriver downward.

Some things, even necessary things, needed to die. Should have died long before.

Let truth become death. Let even the memory be erased.

The lamplight faltered and extinguished. Darkness swept through the attic. The great beast sagged, the gears shifting out of alignment as it leaned forward, carried by his weight, and then Otto was falling and the ground swung toward him. When it hit, he felt ribs snap. Something in his spine popped out of alignment, and he tasted blood. It hurt, but not as badly as he thought it should have hurt. He was too dizzy. He was too tired.

He wanted to look toward the window, but his head wouldn't turn. He couldn't make out the Orloj.

But for a moment, when he looked up into the rafters, he thought he could see something far more marvelous. A sky. Blue, so blue, without a fleck of smoke to stain it. The sky, high above Letna park, reflected in the Vltava. Wind licked his neck and his mother pressed the wheel of a kite into his grip and the line tugged, the red sail heaved its way up, ducking and bucking as it fought the cord that tethered it, as it yearned to race across that royal blue sky and he was a child again and the cord jumped in his hands, pulled almost free of his grip as it tugged upward toward the heavens.

He held on.